This book is a work of fiction. Any references to historical events, real people, or real places are used fictitiously. Other names, characters, places, and events are products of the author's imagination, and any resemblance to actual events or places or persons, living or dead, is entirely coincidental.

All rights reserved, including the right to reproduce this book or portions thereof in any form whatsoever.

Cover Designed by Michael Brulotte
Edited by Kevin Roberts

© 2024

Dedicated to the resilient people and their experiences that inspired this work of fiction.

Flint Ridge

1

It has been half of a century since I have seen my campmates and even though I no longer enjoy the same youthful reflection as I did back then, my memories have just come flooding back in the most overwhelming of ways. As much as I was hesitant to reconnect and relive the trauma from Flint Ridge, my wife insisted that I attend my fiftieth anniversary as a way to let go of a lifelong burden. Even my three grown children encouraged me to catch up with the people who, dare I say, were responsible for shaping the man I am today. Granted, I have intentionally kept my family in the dark about my sordid experiences to preserve the wholesome yet naïve view of their father. I hate to say it, but if it weren't for the delinquents with whom I involuntarily spent that unfaithful summer, I don't believe I would have had the perseverance to lead a life worth living.

Without the trauma that resulted from an ill-advised upbringing, I might have remained oblivious to not only a well-adjusted lifestyle but also to a now privileged outlook on life. Granted, it would be nice to have a film reel filled with endless fond memories of endearing family trips, sacred conversations with a mother or father, or even an ambitious first day of school, but I prefer to embrace my chaotic childhood and reflect on my younger self as nothing more than a disadvantaged kid. We were all disadvantaged in one way or another; most of us who were sent to Flint Ridge had already dedicated ourselves to a life outside the law, identifying as opportunists rather than conformists.

Therefore, you can imagine the discomfort I feel today as I straighten my navy blue polyester tie in preparation for a reunion with said opportunists. Not only would I have never allowed myself to be dressed in what I would have considered to be a snob's uniform, but I would have also directed my utmost disgust toward a man wearing such an accessory. In fact, we would refer to the businessmen walking around downtown as polished pigs. The sensation of the synthetic fabric on my neck does evoke an unmistakable feeling of discomfort, most likely due to a repressed desire to rebel. Still, decades of routinely wearing one on special occasions has turned me into a creature of habit. It is amusing how the direction of one's life shapes how a person perceives what is appropriate and what is unbecoming. Though the fire to question authority still smolders deep, urging me to march to the beat of my own off-tempo drum, its blaze has dwindled down to a bed of embers once I began looking for some unfamiliar normalcy.

    Once my tie was as straight as I could make it (never learning the proper way to fasten a Windsor knot), I leaned toward the closet door of my hotel room, inching my face closer to the vanity mirror that stood in front of me. Humbly, my reflection has not held up over the years, having been defaced by the unforgettable stressors of life. Yet, I still tried my best to see the seventeen-year-old version of me. The wrinkles were deep, the bags under each eye were darkened as if I had smudged charcoal beneath my eyelids, and the little hair I had left atop my head had turned to a blinding white. Riddled with prominent visual indicators of supposed insight into the meaning of life, I also notice that my pale blue eyes had softened in contrast to my hardened outlook. Compared to my younger, brooding self, it as though I had lost the stare of inexperience. What concerned me was whether my old friends would notice the embarrassingly content demeanor resulting from privilege. In case they were not fortunate enough to build a similar life of comfort, I desperately tried to regress to the angsty boy with whom they'd be abe to commiserate. As much as I tried, it was futile; there was no way to recapture the unfortunate way in which I once saw the world. Knowing what I know now, I wish technology could provide me with the means to contact that boy and break the news to him that his self-inflicted outlook was so bleak because he wasn't in a position to accept happiness as a viable choice.

As my inner monologue shouted voices from the past, condemning me for becoming such a dreadfully straight-laced adult, I feared that revisiting my unsavory life would re-open an old wound. After so many years, that wound must have by now turned into a scar, maing it much harder to re-open. Having said that, it does occur to me that I am not as vulnerable or as volatile as a once was, no longer presenting a need to protect myself from a relentless, cruel world. Now equipped with healthy coping mechanisms to evade overwhelming anger and self-hatred, I am ready as I will ever be to relive my demoralizing past.

Buying time to collect my thoughts and retain my composure, I slowly continued to dress. Taking frequent breaks to sip on a beautifully aged scotch befitting of its consumer, I delayed the inevitable by avoiding the final steps of slipping into my meticulously shined shoes. The longer I procrastinated, the longer I would have to convince myself to walk down the hotel corridor leading to the event room where the rest of the Flint Ridge gang would greet me in a multitude of unexpected ways. If I had to wager to a guess, I believe they would react in one of two ways. The first scenario would involve them disregarding my manicured appearance to focus only on the time we spent together, recalling embarrassing anecdotes that took place over the summer before we were thrust into adulthood. The second (more likely) scenario would be the eruption of insults as every one of my insecurities was brought to light, clear enough to be identified, and subsequently berated by the entire lot of aged ne'er-do-wells.

The person I feared the most to reunite with was my closest friend, Finn "Sparky" Thompson. Although our friendship would probably not have blossomed if not for us both being coerced into the confinement of Flint Ridge, I could not have survived without him that summer. Both of us acted as a person who the other could lean upon when the intensity got the best of us, while the rest of the free world seemed to have congregated on a distant planet. Consequently, as one another's guardian, we became inherently judgmental towards one another as a way to keep our hardened demeanor as unrelenting as possible. In an environment where displaying the slightest sign of weakness could result in a physical or verbal assault, I relied on Finn to recite one of his uninhibited, no-holds-barred speeches on the days I did not possess the gumption to appear brave.

"Tears and blood. 2 for the price of 1 if you let those guys see you like this." He'd say confidently to change my depressed mood.

Though his abrupt "pep" talks were not sensitive by today's standards, they were effective. Nevertheless, I did not look forward to hearing my old friend criticize my subjectively weakened appearance due to an old habit of trying to keep me on my toes.

Against my better instinct and the fluttering of nerves in my stomach, feeling as I did in anticipation of spending time with a vivacious Flint Valley girl, I found myself walking out of my hotel room towards the gathering of my long-lost companions. Unable to restrain my feet from creating momentum as they acted more bravely than I felt, I reached the entrance door to the event room. With my glass in hand, only containing one insufficient sip of single malt scotch to act as a magical elixir to cure my social anxiety, I stood in front of the exquisitely detailed doors, just as petrified as the wood itself.

In a final attempt to postpone the inevitable, I took the time to admire the uniquely crafted door as I ran my hand over the many imperfect cracks in the old wood. I continued to observe the mismatched pieces of wood that, if laid separately, would appear aesthetically displeasing, but when combined, assembled into a piece of art. I thought if my life were represented in a physical entity, it would be that door. Each memory and characteristic formed throughout my life can tend to appear as undesirable, like a fist fight with a foe, a developed tone of sarcasm in the face of fear, or a hatred for authority, but collected as a whole, my unique identity formed.

Giving in to a vivid sensory memory, the sight of this remarkable door, and the subsequent transference I had placed on it, brought me back to the spring of 2023 when I was well into my last year as a youth before turning the legal age of eighteen. As if I had been the first person in existence to discover a time portal, the door at the end of my fingertips morphed into the entrance of the city bank located in my hometown. An uncanny sensation rushed over me as I felt the reluctant power to relive the biggest mistakes of my life while being forced to watch myself go about that ill-fated day.

Frozen at the door of my reunion gathering, I no longer

possessed the strength to push open the heavy wooden door, instead using my limited energy to drift away in rumination. Completely cast away in thought, I lost track of time and awareness as I could see my younger self in front of me; I was compelled to watch the movie of my own life, despite the fact I knew how the next tragic scene unfolded. Watching my younger self with an unusual sense of empathy, I experienced the fear that had encapsulated my entire being that day, unable to stop myself from engaging in an act that would define a major part of my past.

Although it was clear how an event like robbing a bank would affect my life in an obviously negative fashion, it is much more difficult to explain how a negative upbringing could lead to committing a felony. When I say that my upbringing was at the very best negative, I must admit that I did not actually have the luxury of a typical upbringing. Without the luxury of parents, I was shared amongst family members like a bad habit, except I was the only habit any one of them could kick. I had basically begun my solitary journey into life as my mother left me in the maternity wing of St. Jude's Hospital to pursue whatever endeavor she felt would bring meaning to her self-destructive lifestyle. Introduced to the world as an abandoned organism needing assistance rather than a miraculous addition to a family deserving of love, I had become involuntarily institutionalized as of my first breath.

Lacking the warmth of a close-knit family, I had no relatives to welcome me into existence, only unattached doctors, nurses, and subsequent social workers. Therefore, I was first shipped to my grandfather's house, where he initially accepted responsibility for me without the forethought to consider his proven inability to raise a child without severe repercussions. You would think a man in his position would consider his three dysfunctional daughters and accept some responsibility for the dysfunctional way they turned out; all plagued by addiction, low self-worth, and criminality. Luckily, I was not in his care long enough to be impacted by his horrible parenting style. In fact, I knew him for such a small period of my life that to this day I still do not his name. For some illogical reason, I believe I've retained a memory from infancy about his preference to be called "Paps," but he was likely just ordering a cheap beer of a similar-sounding name.

Following a short stint with my enthusiastically inept grandfather, I was removed from his squalor by child protective services and relocated to an equally unfit household run by one of my aunts. Aunt Beth was the eldest of all three children, outranking the middle child of the family, Aunt Eleanor, and the youngest daughter, my mother, whom I've been told was nicknamed Christie. My mother's nickname, which is not short for Christina but for Christian (picked by my delusional, booze hound of a grandfather who inexplicably believed it to be a unisex name), was given to her by her mother, who insensitively coined the name due to my mother's protruding belly, resulting from too many name brand cookies.

Although a nickname that makes light of childhood obesity, especially one that is bestowed onto a child by her own parent, is tasteless at best, it was much more flattering that the one my Aunt Beth earned by the age of fifteen. Bethany, also known as Crystal

Beth by the community, was given her nickname after she had developed an affinity for methamphetamines while in the ninth grade. Her highest level of education was actually quite the academic accomplishment in the Wyatt clan. That name had followed her into her adult years and ultimate narcotic-fueled death shortly after receiving me as a houseguest and legal dependent for a total of four grueling months. Thankful for not having to legally identify with the tainted Wyatt surname, a name said only with scorn when whispered on the streets of my old neighborhood, I instead took Beth's husband Perry's last name, Hunter. Granted, there was far from any prestige associated with the Hunter family, I mentally unassociated myself from any ties to him since we were not of blood relation.

I am indebted to the fact that an infant cannot remember downright abusive and traumatic living conditions because I thankfully cannot recollect the few months I had been put under Aunt Beth's care. Only hearing stories of the uninhabitable environment in which I vulnerably lived for a portion of my infancy, I was made aware of my eldest Aunt's unfit parenting styles and the socially deviant company she kept on a regular basis via my next guardian in line, Aunt Eleanor.

Aunt Eleanor, who peculiarly preferred that I call her "Mum" rather than by her rightful title of "Aunt," made little to no sense, especially because I knew very well she was not my mother and our wilting family tree would support my claim. Nevertheless, I was legally bound to Eleanor for much of my unstable childhood, all the while being subjected to her delusion that I was in fact her child.

Grateful for my distanced genealogy from Eleanor, I believe that if I had been her child, my life might have been taken an even worse direction. Although the rumor involving Eleanor and her teenage pregnancy had been one that should not have been recounted to a child in any circumstance, it was nevertheless irresponsibly told to me. This story, either based on vindictive fiction or tragic truth, still haunts me to this day, and I wonder if Eleanor's immoral character would have been as severe as to discard her own baby as mindlessly as throwing out a carton of spoiled milk.

Although the folklore revolving around her teenage abomination never was clarified, it was known that Aunt Eleanor had been unable to conceive a child with Perry due to his participation in a retrospectively shortsighted, yet financially lucrative scientific study as a young man. At the time, he saw little harm in ingesting a newly fabricated fertility drug over the span of a three-week trial for a sum of two thousand dollars, but the lifelong ramifications of the medication had the reverse effect of sterility. Consequently, Uncle Perry had been unable to give Aunt Eleanor the family of which she had always dreamt. Acting as a blessing in disguise, their inability to replicate their DNA proved to be ideal in the eyes of fellow family members, acquaintances, and law enforcement agents, since their reputation was nothing less than criminally deviant.

As I had mentioned, my Aunt Beth's unflattering yet accurate nickname had been stuck to her like a tattoo since she developed a substance abuse problem as a teenager. This may not have been the case if it wasn't for the bad influence of Eleanor. Even though

Eleanor did not consume drugs herself, she never missed an opportunity to use her influence as a cherished younger sister to peer pressure Beth into buying various pills and powders she had acquired from shady older men. Acting as the campus drug kingpin for their high school, Eleanor utilized the facilities to sell an array of stimulants, depressants, and hallucinogens to her fellow under-age classmates. Even the faculty turned a blind eye by giving her the freedom she needed in the schoolyard and forgiving her pathological truancy in exchange for a monthly protection fee.

Using her illicit entrepreneurial talent, Eleanor developed quite a devoted customer base, and just like a resourceful business owner, she began expanding her product mix by introducing new up-and-coming synthetic drugs as they invaded the drug trade. It was at this time that Eleanor met Perry after looking for an experienced local manufacturer who could provide her with an inexpensive form of methamphetamines. She had been looking for a business partner, but also found a love interest who shared her passion for the black market. Having learned a rudimentary way to cook crystal meth from trial and error, using a few over-the-counter items found at the pharmacy and a child's chemistry set, Perry could fill Eleanor's surging demand for the product. In a short time, the two aspiring drug lords combined their compatible talents and flooded the teenage demographic with enough poison to warrant an investigation from federal agents. However, it was before law enforcement could build a substantial case against the couple that Perry's lack of education and knowhow regarding the mixing of dangerously combustible chemicals led to an explosion that left him with a traumatic brain injury and subsequent mental deficiencies.

As a result of his traumatic brain injury, Perry was prone to spontaneous fits of rage, which were usually directed at Eleanor, since she was typically the closest to him, both physically and intimately. She inexplicably stayed by his side for years, even after he was unable to supply the narcotics she needed to make a comfortable yet illegal living. Assuming she felt partially responsible for the accident and took the blame for her partner's impairment, Eleanor allowed herself to be his punching bag. By the time I had arrived in their lives, my aunt and uncle settled into a routine of unprovoked hostility and subsequent physical attacks. Unfortunately, nothing really changed when their orphaned nephew was thrown into the mix of their wildly unhealthy marriage.

Although my memory regarding the first few years spent with Aunt Eleanor and Uncle Perry is unreliable after the accumulation of over five decades of much more vivid and recent memories, I assume that our living arrangement had started off as uncomfortable and violent as it ended. Remembering as early as five years old, even my underdeveloped intuition had been able to detect the abuse that regularly took place between my caretakers. Oddly enough, my uncle's resting demeanor was quite catatonic, never really saying or doing much. Instead, he would just stare blankly at the television as he watched the same daytime gameshows. I suspect he never understood how the games were played or even the value of the prizes won by the contestants, but I gathered the incessant cheering and flashing lights somehow stimulated his lethargic mind.

It helped that Uncle Perry did not physically appear to be

intimidating, instead looking as though he had suffered from muscle atrophy. His limbs were half the width of Eleanor's and the only meat he had on his entire body was a perfectly spherical bulge of fat protruding from his lower abdomen. I guess he drew his strength from that specific area, as the rest of his frame looked weak and malnourished. Especially his upper torso, where his bones would poke through the oversized white t-shirts he would wear on a daily basis, thereby creating the illusion that his chest and back were topographical maps. As I got older, I tended to underestimate his power by imprudently egging him on with threats of retaliation if he were to strike my aunt once more.

"Back off, moron!" I'd say with an unearned tone of confidence.

As if I suffered from some sort of persistent trauma-induced amnesia, I immediately regretted standing up for my battered aunt when my ill-advised taunting acted as a catalyst, turning Perry's stable lethargy into an explosion of aggression.

I have heard some victims of domestic violence state that they happily accepted the consequences of their spouse's hostility if it meant their child would be safe from harm's way, but Eleanor was no such martyr. Perry was surprisingly resourceful when thrown into a frenzy of exaggerated anger; he used to beat me with any object within reach, depending on which area of the house I had aggravated him. In the bathroom, he would use the shower head as a strangulation tool, whereas in the kitchen he preferred to grab a sturdy hold of the steel tea kettle and use it as oversized brass knuckle rings. Whenever he struck me with the tea kettle, Eleanor would look frustrated that I had once again dented it and would say sternly,

"You're gunna pay for that." Never recognizing the figurative meaning of her threat.

In fact, the first time I felt the hot steel of the recently boiled kettle bash against the back of my head at the tender age of nine, it did not hurt as much as the subsequent, more painful blows, as its shape had become mangled, creating a make-shift mould that supported the natural shape of my head.

Once I awoke from the final inflicted blackout many years later, the dried blood that had collected on the stubble of my shaved head indicated that I had been unconscious for quite some time. Feeling queasy from the apparent concussion I had received, I staggered as I brought myself to my feet and stealthily tried to muffle each movement in case Perry was waiting in the shadows for a one-sided round two. Reaching the door frame that connected the kitchen to the living room in our small, one-bedroom inner city home, I peeked timidly around the corner to identify Perry's presence, like a police officer trying to apprehend an armed perpetrator.

My heart skipped a beat as my first glance caught Perry standing in the middle of the room, but then began beating to a normal rhythm once I noticed that the television had been turned on, which meant that he was back in a state of passive incapacitation. I watched as he sat down in the moss-colored velvet armchair, waiting for his head to droop down to his chest, signaling that he was no longer a threat. Meanwhile, Eleanor sat on the adjacent couch with a lit cigarette, oblivious to the recent attack on her only nephew; choosing not to acknowledge my presence as I walked across the living room floor, where the linoleum flooring might as well have been made out of hundreds of fragile eggshells. Passing in front of the television, Perry's head lifted slightly as I obstructed the view of whatever pseudo-entertainment he had apparently been enjoying, but then returned to its resting state as I cleared past his narrow field of vision and walked out the door.

Before I could leave, my aunt's shrill voice raised the blonde hairs on the back of my neck as she demanded in an unnecessarily loud tone that I go to the store to purchase her another carton of cigarettes to last her the remainder of the evening.

"Kid, smokes!" She'd bellow across the room.

Insincerely obliging what sounded not even slightly like a request, I then led her to believe that I would return from the corner store shortly. Never returning to that house, I instead chose a path that would soon lead to summer at Flint Ridge and ultimately bring me to this very hotel, where I now stand too nervous to partake in this dreaded reunion.

Feeling a phantom pain on the back of my skull, reminiscent of the last time Perry struck me with a kitchen appliance, I removed my hand from the beautifully crafted hotel door and rubbed the scar. Guiding my fingers over the healed wound, like I was reading a haunting book written in braille, it told the story of the final act of child abuse that led to my decision to leave the dangerous house I first called home.

2

As unusual as it might seem to lean on the past as a way of avoiding the present, my recollection of past events is as vivid and retrievable as if they were happening in real-time. Perhaps it's a defence mechanism, where I feel more in control of already-formed memories than live in the present, risking the possibility of creating new undesirable ones. Comforted by my ability to take the reins of my focus, I once again immersed myself in the past, deflecting the unknown that awaited me on the other side of the door.

Drawn back to seeing the world through seventeen-year-old eyes, I remember seeing the cul-de-sac with unbelievably accurate detail as I walked away from the house that was cluttered with wall-to-wall agony, hoarding sentiments of hurt and resentment. I picked up my pace down the street, trying to keep my scuffed white thrift store sneakers from being left in my tracks with no laces to hold them on my feet. With every hurried step I took, I was able to take an extra breath of relief as I distanced myself from the cage that housed my abusive uncle and enabling aunt. I did not yet know how I would liberate myself from the confines of that torturous dwelling but I was committed to exhausting all options before crawling back to humbly receive my nightly beating.

Once I had made it no more than four blocks away from the house, I heard a familiarly breaking voice yell as the person rapidly approached me from behind.

"Incoming!" The pubescent voice said.

Before I could turn around to greet my younger next-door neighbor, Joe "Lucky" Conners, whose ironic nickname was appointed to him as a misnomer, picked up speed on his low-rider BMX bike and swiped my legs from underneath me with the baseball bat he had always carried with him. Sending me on my back, I lost my balance from the unanticipatedly swift crack to the back of my knees and landed on my back, once again hitting my head in the exact spot the tea kettle bashed earlier that day. I laid on the ground, incapacitated by the throbbing pain that radiated from the back of my neck, all the way down my spine, which caused a series of sharp impulses in my shoulders and lower back. I wasted little time dwelling on my physical distress and jumped on to my feet to kick Lucky off his bike, continuing to laugh at my misfortune as he was propelled to the uneven pavement.

"Lucky, you asshole! I said out of equal parts anger and pain.

"Damn, due. Don't be a spaz." Lucky said annoyingly before brushing off dirt from his ripped jeans.

Satisfied with my retaliation, a smirk formed on my face as I watched Lucky's frustrated expression follow his prized bicycle roll directly into one of the many deep potholes of the city street, bending the spokes as the front wheel collided with the solid edge of the asphalt. Visibly hurt from his own collision with the rough concrete, he stayed true to the way boys in our neighborhood masked their pain. Displaying a disingenuous sense of invincibility, he strutted over to his damaged bike without so much as brushing off the gravel that had been lodged in his elbows. As gang tattoos indicate allegiance to a group of rough-and-tumbles, we all had lacerations on our elbows and knees from a combination of dilapidated housing and poorly executed stunts on stolen bikes and skateboards. Even though a trickle of blood started to run down his left elbow from the wound inflicted by hitting it against the cracked sidewalk, his attention was directed at retrieving his bike, which then prompted a string of passionately enunciated expletives.

"Fucker, man! Jesus fuckin' Christ, dude!" He muttered under his breath.

Lucky had a very limited vocabulary and rarely found the need to express himself using multisyllabic words.

Unable to ride his bike due to the imbalance created by the bent spokes and cracked tire rim, he decided to push it as he continued to limp alongside. I began to walk faster hoping that Lucky's oblivious mind would pick up on the social cue I was blatantly directing toward him. However, it was lost on him; he continued to push his bike as it made an infuriatingly consistent metallic clicking noise every time the warped rim spun through the narrow forks of the bike's front end.

Amidst his perpetual cursing, he cut his crude story of watching Kelly Stetson, an exquisitely blossoming girl who caught the hormone-riddled eye of every boy in town, through her bedroom window that morning as she tried on her new skin tight jeans. Bragging about the opportune positioning of his kitchen window to that of Kelly's bedroom, I interrupted his unprovoked detailed anecdote by questioning his motivation to engage in such deviant behavior, in his parents' kitchen no less.

"You need help, man. Serious, court-ordered help," I said

with conviction.

Caught off guard by my attention to his absent-minded divulgence of humiliating detail, he quickly changed the subject with a stammering segue, averting my attention to the dried blood on the back of my head.

"What happened back there?" he said.

Knowing the answer to his obvious observation, Lucky rambled off a scenario illustrating his grandiose perception of his own strength, pointing out that he would have left Perry sobbing after feeling his supposed wrath. Although he didn't put it so eloquently, I find it unnecessary to repeat his colorful language. Despite Lucky's tough demeanor, the only true sentiment he had ever felt was terror, masked by an overbearing portrayal of confidence, just as any other boy in our neighborhood who endured abuse from at least one malicious guardian. We were alike in the sense that we were tired of feeling like our homes, which should have felt like a haven from the unwelcoming character that embodied our streets, were just as dangerous and much more unforgiving.

Lucky fantasized about various outlandish scenarios that always ended with him being allowed to leave his house and miserably drunken father behind, such as winning the lottery despite never buying a single lottery ticket, being discovered by an extreme sports talent scout despite having literally no talent in any sport ever invented, or robbing a bank of its millions despite his debilitating fear of disciplinary consequences. No matter how the windfall would actualize, Lucky would always end his fantasy by saying in a hopeful tone,

"Then I'm outta here forever."

He must have repeated each scenario a thousand times before that day but for some reason, the third hypothetical get-rich-quick scheme resonated with me and was not ignored.

I challenged my dimwitted friend's empty promise by questioning the particulars of his plan.

"Oh yeah?" I said inquisitively, "How would that work?"

Flattered by my interest, he explained that he would wait until 12:05 p.m. before entering the bank's lobby since the elderly security guard, Stan, took his daily lunch break like clockwork at noon, who would take at least four minutes to shuffle off the premises to grab a coffee and half of a salami sandwich at the unsanitary, yet frequently visited *Delectable Delicatessen*. He continued to share the plans of his foolproof heist by stating that once Stan, who was in fact armed with an unauthorized .38 caliber revolver he had brought from home was out of sight, he would be able to waltz up to Craig Wellerman, the only bank teller employed by the prestigious city bank, and order him to empty the vault.

Little did he know, despite the overwhelming evidence that the bank in our poverty-stricken town was itself facing bankruptcy and was not even equipped with a vault. However, Lucky's unrealistic impression that every bank in the country was overflowing with gold bricks and hundred dollar bills from the depictions in one too many Hollywood bank robbery movies, had taken over his ability to consider alternate conclusions.

Once Lucky had excitedly finished reciting the robbery he

had envisioned every night after acting as his father's weathered punching bag, I was overcome with an unfamiliar sense of praise for his half-baked idea.

"Let's do it!" I said impulsively.

Taken aback by my enthusiasm with his plan, he dropped his treasured bike to the ground and left it behind without a thought, assuming that he would soon amass a large fortune, no longer bound to a broken bicycle he had to steal from a junkyard. Enthralled by my cooperation, he directed me on the path to the nearby bank where we would quickly enact our poorly planned-out scheme, then immediately start a lavish life of independence far from any individual who wished us harm. As we approached the bank, Lucky reached into the deep pocket of his poorly fitted, excessively long jean shorts and pulled out an intimidatingly large chrome pistol.

He said with a patronizing tone, "Take this. You need it more than I do."

Then handed me the pistol and assured me that his father wouldn't realize it was gone until he woke up from his bourbon-induced evening nap. This would give us two to three hours to flee, by which point we would be far past the city limits and on our way to a life of finer things. Feeling entitled to the life we expected to be living later that day, we looked forward to the long overdue retroactive pay for seventeen years of hardship. As such, we embraced the life choice and disregarded any consequences that might follow armed robbery. Initially reluctant to handle the stolen pistol, I eventually agreed to be the gunman after Lucky assured me that his father had wasted all of the rounds on dusty liquor bottles the night before, and that I was in no imminent danger of unloading the lethal lead on unsuspecting Craig Wellerman. Satisfied by the fact that the gun was apparently a mere prop in our performance rather than a tool capable of murder, I confidently held onto the grip of the gun in my right hand and began to run full steam toward the bank.

As we came around the adjacent corner, we could see that Stan the geriatric security guard was well on his way to the deli for his lunch break, which meant we were free to accept our destiny and take our dues with force. I approached the wooden door and placed my empty left hand on the tarnished handle as Lucky nervously stood behind me, acting as an frazzled lookout. Swinging the heavy door open, the glare from the noon sun distorted my vision, obscuring the dim lobby of the bank to the point where I could not see a foot in front of me, let alone the positioning of Craig the bank teller. Acting out of agitation and adrenaline, I raised the gun and pointed it toward whatever or whoever stood in front of me in the dark establishment. As my eyes started to focus, the silhouette of a mysterious figure approached me at an unsettlingly brisk rate, to which I was reflexively pulled the trigger on the supposedly empty gun.

The never-before-heard booming sound of an echoing gunshot ringed in my deafened ears as I was overcome with an instant sense of regret and remorse toward the unknown figure I had impulsively shot. Assuming I had fired at Craig, my stomach sank thinking about the two recently orphaned daughters we would leave behind due to my unprovoked act of aggression. I was overcome with guilt knowing that Mrs. Wellerman had succumbed to breast cancer the previous winter and was missed by all, most of all by her grieving family. To think that I had demolished an already broken family led me to want to end my life right then and there. Experiencing my first sentiment of genuine remorse, I was relieved to see Craig huddled down in the corner of the bank as my eyes adjusted to the artificial lighting, shaking from the audible gunfire but untouched by the hot lead I had released into the lobby.

Noticing that the bank was empty expect for the traumatized bank teller, my fears, intertwined with debilitating and self-loathing guilt, were washed away by a tsunami of relief. Realizing that I had received an unanticipated second chance following a ridiculously flawed plan, I turned to Lucky to prompt him to run away as I had intended to do,

"Let's go, man!" I said impatiently.

But, when I looked behind me all I could see is Stan with his arms positioned straight out towards me in anticipation that I would turn the gun on him.

"Don't shoot." He said almost in a whimper.

Dropping the pistol to the ground, I hoped that the careless manipulation of a loaded weapon would literally not backfire. My hands raised as my eyes followed the falling revolver down to where Lucky was laying immobilized with a pool of streaming garnet-colored blood from the back of his head, located in the exact same spot where I had been hit with Eleanor's tea kettle earlier that day. Due to similarly unfortunate circumstances, both Lucky and myself had been enticed into committing a criminal act that day, neither of us having the foresight to consider the fatal consequences. The randomness that yields from a mind-boggling universe led Lucky down a dead-end, whereas I was given the chance to see the error of my intentions.

3

Fixated on the lifeless stare of Lucky's inanimate face, I was finally overcome with grief from my traumatizing past and felt as though the anxiety experienced in the present could not hold a candle to the morose woes of the past. Therefore, I was ready to take the plunge into the bizarre reunion to voluntarily socialize with a group of juvenile delinquents I once resented. I then pushed against the heavy wood door and submissively glanced around the party with my head pointed towards the floor in hopes that no one would recognize my visibly aged face.

Confused by the reception of my delayed entrance into the hotel event room, I was overwhelmed with a satisfying sense of relief once I realized I was the first to arrive. As I collected my composure by lifting my head to a normal and less straining angle, I veered my sights around each hidden corner before basking in some much-appreciated solitude. I should have expected as much seeing as how the invitees had all at one time been notorious for disregarding instruction and acting on self-interest rather than common courtesy. Noticing yet another indication of how I had matured into a man, I somehow had become socially aware enough to be respectful of the others' time. As the self-praise quickly faded, I realized that being the first guest to arrive would warrant even more jeers from my unrelenting peers.

    Growing exhausted from my learned coping mechanism of dwelling on predicting the unpredictable facts of the future, I decided to divert my attention to the buffet table that looked to have been recently set up by hotel staff. Walking over to the condensation-dripping chrome lids that covered various comfort foods, I paid little attention to the party etiquette my wife felt compelled to teach me following one too many awkward dinner parties involving my stuffed face, her overt humiliation, and disgruntled hosts. Helping myself, I lifted each of the chrome lids and indiscriminately began loading an ornately designed ceramic plate with gold trim to its maximum capacity with hefty portions of food I would later have to explain to my cardiologist with shame. I then scooped an assortment of of double-battered deep fried chicken, bacon wrapped wieners dripping with maple syrup, dense Swedish meatballs drenched in a heavy gravy, and over stuffed chicken cordon bleu oozing with savory mozzarella and salted ham.

    Once my plate had reached a substantial weight warranting two trembling hands to support the smorgasbord of delectably rich entrees, I closed each of the four chrome lids after rearranging the remaining feast in a fashion that would not bring attention to the many missing pieces. I then made my way to the nearest table in case I needed to revisit the buffet in an urgently timely manner, where I had my choice of elegantly rustic-decorated white chairs. Looking down at the mountain of oddly paired, yet somehow appetizing food, I ignored the functional purpose of the cutlery wrapped in a cloth napkin that had been provided at each place setting. Instead of opting to use my fingers to shovel the hot greasy mess into my mouth, I used my tongue to wipe up the excess sauce that had run down my finger that collected in a pool surrounding my wedding ring, then overflowed into the crevasse of my wrist. Before I could stop to enjoy the eclectic flavors I had introduced to my palate, it appeared that my plate was void of delicious foods, prompting concern as to how I was physically able to gorge without remembering to take a single breath.

    Since I had consumed an unhealthy amount of comfort food in record-breaking time, an act that would undoubtedly gain the respect of professional hot dog contest eaters around the world, I was left once again to stir in the anxiety of tasking myself welcoming former Flint Ridge residents. Realizing that a guest could arrive at any moment, I quickly removed my impressively clean plate and straightened the table cloth to give the illusion that I had not succumbed to my gluttonous fault. Faced with a predicament that may very well reveal my nonexistent will power towards fatty foods, I did not know what to do with my plate as there wasn't any receptacle to deposit the shameful piece of ceramic. Unwilling to open myself up to even more ridicule by leaving it at the vacant table, I gave myself two equally uncouth options to effectively mask my selfish act. I had to choose between placing the plate that had been cleaned by my unsterilized tongue at the bottom of the pile of clean plates on the buffet table or inconspicuously tossing the plate in the covered garbage bin on the other side of the room, with the intention of leaving a generous twenty-dollar bill on the nightstand in my hotel room as reimbursement. Since I did not have the heart to potentially subject an old acquaintance to an unsanitary dinner plate, I walked to the other end of the room and dropped the plate in the garbage as if I had been instructed to do so by a bizarre ransom note. Unfortunately, I had not anticipated the velocity at which the plate would fall into the metal container, causing a startlingly audible crash that must have been heard from inside the kitchen once the shatter of ceramic echoed through the once deathly silent banquet hall.

Standing as though I was a fawn exposed to rapidly nearing high beams on a country road, I waited in one place to see if I would be held accountable for my rash actions. Nervous to make another sound, I feared that the fresh rubber on the soles of my newly purchased dress shoes would call the attention of a concerned hotel staff member. Although I considered running as fast as my unathletic body could to escape the humiliation of being linked to an overthought act of hotel property destruction, the absence of noise led me to believe there would be no investigation into the abrupt crashing. Allowing myself to walk away from the veritable crime scene, I walked back to my original resting spot and pulled out the chair to wait for guests to arrive.

Having just implicated myself in petty hotel property destruction, acting as carelessly as an out-of-control rockstar, I sat in my chair with perfect posture simultaneously feeling undesirable sentiments of guilt and anxiety as to how the night would pan out. Ironically, these two comorbid feelings were those I felt on the escorted bus ride to Flint Ridge fifty years prior. Even though I feel comfortable in my suit and tie, I immediately started to squirm in my seat feeling the government-issued one-sized white crewneck t-shirt and black cotton sweatpants I wore for my two-hour road trip to the Flint Ridge Juvenile Detention Camp. And just like that, my mind had forced me back to a time when I felt like my future was about to be short-lived.

In the months leading up to that dreaded bus ride, I was subject to a lengthy trial that reviewed my involvement in the events that surrounded Lucky Conners' death. I was swiftly punished for my intent to commit robbery by being sentenced to a summer at Flint Ridge. Flint Ridge is the setting where countless young offenders are emotionally broken down and given time to reflect on poor life decisions. Intended to serve the same purpose in my situation, the judge expressed concern about my cold and apparent psychopathic demeanor when I resisted my overwhelming emotions by holding back tears when the court discussed the details of Lucky's murder. He insisted out of his responsibility to uphold the safety of his community, that Flint Ridge would provide me with some much-needed discipline before becoming a legal adult, before being susceptible to serious imprisonment in a federal correctional facility.

"You got lucky this time, kid." He said not realizing the ironic insensitivity of his word choice. "Next time, you won't be given any leeway."

Although the words and ruling of the judge were inferred as undeserved and exaggerated by my underdeveloped mind, I now sympathize with his idealist intentions and wish the social programs in place at the time had been structured in a way to support the supposed intent of the judicial system.

Naïvely resentful of the judge's hasty sentencing, I sat alone in the correctional department's exhaust-filled bus, stewing in anger as a guard watched over me with an intimidating stare. He cautiously stood over the bus driver's shoulder in case I tried to overpower the armed officer in a futile attempt to seek freedom from incarceration. Although it did cross my mind to attempt liberating myself from transport to what could only be a government-run hell in the hills, I remembered back to the last time I let my imagination direct the course of my life and figured it could only end badly. The only positive emotion I felt during that overheated, rocky bus ride was the satisfying realization that I would not have to spend the summer acting as a chopping block whenever Perry's sadistic attention was led astray as summer re-runs fell short as an effective distraction.

As the perspiration collected on my brow, I was no longer able to endure the effects of the blazing summer's sun on the oven-on-wheels, provoking me to aggressively threaten the hardened guard to turn on the air-conditioning before I reported him to the human rights office for child abuse.

"I know my rights," I said inaccurately. "and you're violating them."

Knowing that my threats were unsubstantiated since there was no such office in that particular jurisdiction, the smug guard allowed a smirk to transform his previously hostile face, then reached down to his side and retrieved a bottle of cola that had only a sip taken from it. Thinking I had forced his hand by jeopardizing his job, I leaned back in my seat to accept my cold drink and exude my dominance on my physically and socially superior escort. As he approached with a confidence that should have triggered skepticism regarding his improbable compliance, I held out my hand with minimal effort to make him bend over and place the plastic bottle in my shackled hand. Waiting with an unmerited arrogance as the statuesque guard twisted off the cap of the once carbonated beverage, he proceeded to pour the contents of the heated soft drink over my head, shaking every last drop of the sticky sun-drenched liquid to flow through the stubble on my shaved head.

"That oughta cool you off, boy," he said with a gravelly voice.

My blood boiled from the thermally equivalent soda that washed over my head and down my shoulders, creating a molasses-type adhesive, bonding my skin to the rough blend of synthetic fabrics of my cola-stained t-shirt. In response to the humiliating, not to mention uncomfortable gesture, I let my reactive emotions outweigh rationale as I subtly linked my two restrained hands at the knuckles to make a solid fist, then swung at the guard's face with every ounce of rage-fueled aggression. Forgetting that my ankles had also been shackled to the floor of the bus, my limited mobility only allowed me to raise from the seat a couple of inches before retracting to my original position. My locked palms had fallen short from the guard's face, but the intent of action itself had been clear to the domineering guard, prompting him to use his free range of motion and superior strength to strike me square in the face, leaving a decent sized, bloody gash at the top of my nose.

"Tough guy, aren't ya?" He cackled.

Having been aggressively adorned with what looked like a dark and twisted tye-dye shirt, the dark cola and bright red blood that streamed from the open wound between my eyes swirled on the collar of my loose-fitting shirt. That single blow to the bridge of my nose was a clear indicator of how the staff at Flint Ridge dealt with disobedience, adhering to a strict zero-tolerance policy when faced with confrontational behavior. As much as I still resent the guards as a collectively violent staff, I can now view the situation with the slightest (minuscule, even) bit of understanding to ascertain what intimidating events must have transpired in order to adopt corporal punishment. There is no doubt in my mind that the protection of the staff's physical well-being became a necessity well before it became excessive force. Since many of the like-minded campers at Flint Ridge were possessed with the same learned hatred for authority, they evoked danger in the eyes of their enforcers and demanded retaliation when displaying harmful, even life-threatening, behaviors.

Humbled by the unforeseen attack, I refrained from speaking another word to the explosive guard even though my body and mind were working in productive cohesion in case I chose to retaliate. My entire body was shaking in anticipation of returning the strike, ready to fight back at the drop of my shackles, while my mind was flooded with enough adrenaline to sufficiently numb any subsequent blows I would receive from the robust guard. However, I simply stewed in my seat until my instinctual response to fight subsided. To be clear, it was not the perfectly landed punch that prompted my passivity, but rather my fear of what unknown hell he was capable of putting me through for the rest of the ninety-two days at Flint Ridge. Just in case I were to arouse his need to release some physical angst, I locked my eyes on the window next to me. I was not ready to trigger a fit of rage on account of a perceived dirty look, since I was indeed aware that my facial expressions could speak volumes to my mood and practically shout every thought that crossed my mind.

I had become no stranger to violence; in fact, it was a daily challenge. Engaging in such a challenge was to establish my dominance over rambunctious neighbor kids who turned to brawls as a way of transferring their anger directed at their abusive father or mother. I have heard that in other inner-city neighborhoods, the tormented children used dancing to express their despair, acting as an effective form of physical release. This may be so, but the kids in my neighborhood were unfortunately not as musically inclined or disciplined enough to learn a creative craft, such as dance. Therefore, we turned to fighting: an equally effective, not to mention, safer way of channeling our aggression. Most of us found that letting off steam on each other by engaging in fist fights on the streets and in parks was the wiser choice given our circumstances. Rather than foolishly allowing our anger to surface during a beating from a parent or relative who was capable of inflicting much more pain and causing much more severe injuries, we could burn off excess negative energy and pass the time with a heated gathering of our peers.

Brawls would take place on most nights in the alleys and abandoned parks of my neighborhood. Due to the high demand for violence, there was never a need to schedule a match or invite an audience to cheer on the fighters as they were always an abundance of blood-thirsty spectators. If you couldn't find an altercation between at least two mentally unstable, hormonally driven teenagers, that would be because you were trying your best to ignore it. Adapting to street fighting as a way of dealing with strife at home was, at first, a demanding feat due to my small size, standing modestly at nearly five and a half feet, weighing a maximum of one hundred and forty pounds (if I were to be weighed fully dressed with my jean pockets filled to the brim with rocks). Granted, I have now put on a significant amount of weight over fifty years of stress eating, but I still to this day do not appear in any way, shape, or especially form, athletic or intimidating. Due to my unfortunately small frame, I was initially seen as an easy target for boys much larger than myself to project their feelings of inadequacy. They saw me as a quick release to throw one or two punches, then walk away feeling vindicated while I lay defeated on the ground. Admittedly, this was how the first seven to ten encounters transpired over the course of my initiation into high school. That is, until I found a way to use my compact size to swiftly maneuver around my opponent.

    Making up for a lack of strength with speed and agility, my ability to duck and slip around my sizeable opponent was initially used as an avoidance tactic rather than a strategy to retaliate. At first, my main concern was to leave unscathed and return home without any open wounds on my face as it made my uncle's job much easier to draw blood, thus bringing him an undeserved sense of satisfaction. However, once I realized that the larger boys were incapable of anticipating my next move, I started mustering enough courage to throw a punch when the opportunity presented itself – usually aimed at the lower back. Since I had very little power behind my underdeveloped body, my strategy was to hit often, not hard. Swiftly hitting my attacker as many times as possible was an effective way of disorienting him, thereby losing balance and eventually bringing him to his knees where I could then strike effectively to end the fight. After gaining experience with daily confrontations, my accuracy improved, as did my strength, which gave me the athletic edge in the competition. By the time I reached Flint Ridge, the scars on my knuckles outnumbered the ones on my face.

Although I felt confident to hold my own and deliver a fair fight if given the opportunity to confront the overcompensating guard, I was not willing to endure any subsequent pain at the expense of an underestimation. Instead, I chose to distract myself from the intense throbbing pressure that radiated from what felt like a broken nose by taking in the rural scenery. If anything, it would provide me with the basic knowledge of the landscape in case I had to escape from the camp at some point that summer. As much as I would have never admitted this to any of my fellow incarcerated campers at Flint Ridge, I was captivated by the nature that surrounded the country road leading up to Flint Ridge. Aesthetically invigorating, it reminded me of an old country song that Eleanor would play at full volume to drown out the disturbingly loud grunts of Perry's fit of rage as he assaulted me.

Raised in a concrete habitat, I had never in my life seen so much greenery. The most vegetation I had seen was the community garden located on the roof of my old high school, grown by a local not-for-profit organization to provide us, low-income children, with a sliver of carrot or chunk of cucumber with our government-funded lunch. It was astonishing to see how many colors existed in nature, realizing for the first time in seventeen years that there was an entire world on the outskirts of the pavement and steel-laden reality to which I had grown accustomed. Despite the shackles and obstructed airway, being surrounded by untouched landscapes induced an unfamiliar sense of freedom, allowing me to breathe a breath of relief. Perhaps it was just a refreshing change of scenery, but I never wanted that rocky bus ride to end. I wished at that moment for the driver to keep on driving down a rural route and follow the tree line indefinitely. Even the sadistic guard on board no longer bothered me, he was temporarily disregarded along with every other problem I had floating away in the stormy seas of my mind.

 Taking myself on a brief vacation through the forests leading up to Flint Ridge, I nearly forgot about the destination. For an instant, I led myself to believe I was on a summer vacation with a loving family headed to our favorite camping spot. This delightful delusion was abruptly cut short when I caught a glimpse of the Flint Ridge Juvenile Detention Camp sign growing nearer from outside the bug-spattered windshield. Only averting my attention from the window for a split second to continue avoiding eye contact with the guard, who looked as though he needed some action to cure the boredom resulting from a long bus ride, I was unnerved by the fast-approaching, rusted metal sign made holy by what I assumed to be stray bullets. Half expecting there to be a large wooden arch carved with bold branded letters spelling out the name of the camp as I had seen in so many summer camp movies, I was wildly disappointed to see a chipped yellow road sign indicating that the camp was less than a mile ahead. Acting more as a warning sign to motorists than a welcoming tourist information guide, I wish I could turn the bus around and find a more relaxing vacation spot.

    Reaching a Texas gate nearly a mile past the warning sign, the bus driver barely slowed down, causing the seat to shake uncontrollably, jostling the metal cuffs against my already skinned wrists and ankles. Once we cleared the ineffective speed trap, we stopped about fifty feet from an industrial-sized swinging gate, adorned with ample amounts of barbed wire and rusted steel spears. Unsettled by the intimidatingly secure entrance, feeling as though I was about to enter either an internment camp or nature reserve for prehistoric animals, I was overwhelmed with panic as the bus driver leaned out of his narrow window to scan an electronic pass, triggering the slow-moving maximum security gate to creek toward the bus. Only slightly missing the bumper of the bus, I was sure the motorized monstrosity was going to make contact with the vehicle, making it apparent that the intention was to leave as little room as possible for intruders to enter or involuntarily-held guests to leave. Seconds after the gate had fully opened, the bus began to roll forward, prompting the gate to close immediately behind; this time swiping the rear, causing a shattering sound, prompting the guard and bus driver to curse in unison at the sound of a broken taillight. The gate had slammed shut behind us, securely locking into place as the next shipment of troubled youth was held against their will at Flint Ridge. There was no turning back at this point, my fear had become reality and the consequences of my most recent life choices presented themselves to be endured.

4

Clearly remembering that dirt road entrance to Flint Ridge, I did not know what to expect or how tolerable my stay would be, but had an ominous paranoia. Is paranoia in fact paranoia if in retrospect it was justified, or is it simply a keen sense of perception? Either way, any sense of optimism was fleeting. Once the bus pulled up to the doors of the main hall, looking like a Victorian mansion manufactured with scavenged redwood logs and crude mud-like, brownish-grey cement, there was no indication as to how my arrival would be received. From what I could see, there wasn't a soul roaming around the grounds, except for a well-dressed middle-aged man walking forward in response to the engine back-fire. The guard instructed me to keep my hands to myself as he released the latch that connected my limbs to the floor below, then roughly grabbed me by the inside of my bicep to escort me off the bus. Before I stepped foot off the bus that acted as a brief safe haven, I wished I could stay shackled to the fantasy of traveling on a vacation rather than to that dreary reality. Unfortunately, this was no vacation and the misery of Flint Ridge would be felt from the instant my foot touched its soil.

Stepping towards the unknown man, I suspected he oversaw the camp as he was dressed far better than the guards; sporting a charcoal suit with a bright white pocket square on his chest. If I hadn't known any better, I would have guessed that Mother Nature was trying to give me one last chance to escape as a strong wind came between us, rustling the previously still trees and propelling the sand and gravel from the ground at high speeds. Barely able to see the man standing but a foot in front of me, I only noticed that the eyeglasses sitting atop his head had blown off, tumbling down on the gravel. As I instinctually bent down to retrieve the man's glasses for him, my simple act of kindness was met with a stinging slap to the back of my head. Thrusting me forward from the momentum of the unprovoked slap, the weight of my body bent the thin-framed glasses and crushed both lenses. Confused as to what I had done to receive punishment for being a decent human being, I stood up from the gravel with glass and rocks protruding from the palm of my hand while my head started to ache. Above me, I could hear an usually soft-spoken man say,

"Such acts of disobedience is not tolerated here at Flint Ridge."

My first assumption that the swift blow had come from the guard, who had proven his quick response to violence on the bus ride to the camp, proved to be wrong after hearing the stern yet eloquent voice. I was shocked when I looked up at the disheveled well-dressed man as he wiped off his red hand with a white handkerchief. Expressing inexplicable hostility towards me, the slender man agitatedly brushed the bangs from his eyes back to where they had been laying before the wind re-styled it, then exclaimed,

"You do not have the right to touch a staff member's

personal property, let alone the personal property of the Camp Director."

Irritated by my reflex to pick up an object that had fallen to the ground, he continued to threaten,

"Perhaps you would benefit from the discipline found only in a federal penitentiary. Would that suit you better?"

Waiting for a response to his supposedly rhetoric yet plausible question, he coerced me to give him a simple head nod to make it clear that I understood he wasn't a man to take lightly. Although I was fairly certain the power that came with the title of Camp Director didn't come close to that of a judge, I recognized the man's desire to prove a point and establish his dominance. Since I wasn't in a position to question his authority without inflicting more pain upon myself, I ignored the overwhelming disrespect I had for his domineering demeanor and followed his lead into the administrative building.

Refraining from uttering a single word or gesturing in any way that wasn't indicative of a subdued prisoner, I walked with an imbalanced saunter behind the Camp Director as my feet were still tied together. The man walked forward, never looking back to speak to me face-to-face, and then finally introduced himself as Mr. Desmond, subsequently reiterating his self-proclaimed vanity title. I found it quite insulting that he had the audacity to raise a hand to me before I even knew his name; perhaps protocol relating to abuse differed at Flint Ridge, but where I came from it was basic decency to introduce yourself well before hitting a perfect stranger. We didn't have much in terms of dignity in my old neighborhood, but at least we valued accountability and respect.

As my tour of Flint Ridge continued, I was still baffled by the absence of individuals wearing similar attire to my own. Through the main hall, I was informed of various staff members' roles and names, but not one inmate. My curiosity got the best of me and outweighed my aversion to being hit again (since my nose and head were pounding in excruciating unison), so I asked Mr. Desmond with an ill-advised sarcastic tone,

"Where are the other inmates? Or am I was the only privileged guest at Flint Ridge?"

Expecting another corrective blow to my head, Mr. Desmond surprised me by continuing to walk straight forward without as much as lifting his hands from his pockets. Instead, he replied in a stern voice,

"The term "inmate" isn't used here at Fint Ridge. We instead like to view our guests as campers. Has a nice ring to it, does it not?"

Despite the polished term that was most likely implemented in hopes of deterring the "campers" from inferring a prolonged sense of criminality, thereby reducing the chance of becoming institutionalized, I still felt more like an inmate. I thought realistically to myself as to how many campers wore shackles and doubted it would be an enticing amenity to advertise on a brochure for parents to consider when choosing the perfect summer camp for their precious children.

Following Mr. Desmond's sugar-coated labeling of Flint Ridge's involuntarily held adolescents, I still did not receive insight regarding the rest of the camp's delinquent population. Despite my sustained interest, I was not willing to test my luck by questioning the short-tempered man again, and assumed we would come across the holding area soon enough. Keeping quiet, we continued our riveting administrative building tour, where I was shown two points of interest.

First, I was escorted through the intake office where my photo was taken by an elderly lady with a chronic cough and unsteady hands unfit for camera work, which was to be placed on an identification badge that I was obligated to wear at all times without exception. Confused as to whether the life-long smoker had been speaking out of habit or had a sick sense of humor, but before snapping my mug shot she said in a raspy voice,

"Smile, kid."

Following her direction, she captured a less than flattering photo of blood-stained teeth. In fact, I still have that badge in a cardboard box my wife inexplicably marked "Memories" with a black marker. I'm not sure if that keepsake is disingenuous or a misguided heartfelt gesture.

Second, we visited the nursing station equipped with one nurse in the "rare" case I needed medical attention over the course of the summer. Due to bad timing, the nurse was absent that day and could not tend to the wounds I had recently been given as a welcoming gift to Flint Ridge. Noting the injuries I had sustained within the first hours of being under the camp staff's supervision, Mr. Desmond advised me to contact a bunker Counselor if I felt the need to return the next day to meet with Nurse Bea for a stitch or two. In response to the director's snide comment, my friendly guard motioned his fist to uppercut my chin, then pulled back in laughter as I flinched. Apparently bullies aren't restricted to the schoolyard.

Once we reached the exit of the first building, quickly becoming one of the least hospitable tours I had ever been on, Mr. Desmond scanned his card on a key pad allowing access to leave through the back door. Venturing into the back of the unnecessarily large structure with only two visible purposes, I stood on the edge of a large unmaintained grassy area measuring no more than an acre, surrounded by three long cabins that were built alongside the slope of a rocky ridge. I was instructed that the two cabins on the far sides of the uncut field were the bunkers in which all campers would sleep: the one on the left was Bunker Seven and the one on the right was Bunker Eight. I was told that since I was seventeen, I would be assigned to Bunker Eight for the older boys aged fifteen to seventeen, whereas Bunker Seven was reserved for the youngest boys aged twelve to fourteen. It was also brought to my attention that I would be the most senior camper that summer with my eighteenth birthday right around the corner. Alluding to the suggestion that I act as a good example for my bunkmates, even though I was sure armed robbery was not one of the lesser charges leading to an all-expense vacation at Flint Ridge..

While warden Desmond continued to recite details about the stellar accommodations located at Flint Ridge, I allowed myself to get lost in thought and figured I could gather any pertinent information I had missed later on when needed. I fixated on Bunker Seven and how there was a need to house boys between the age of twelve and fourteen. Granted, I could have used some discipline or even an escape from my hostile environment at that young age, but it was still difficult to fathom how life could be led astray at such a typically innocent age. It is even harder to believe that the pre-teen residents of Bunker Seven are now well into their sixties, but I'm sure if any one of them walks through the banquet hall room for this reunion, I will still look at them through woeful eyes. As we walked past Bunker Seven, I imagined seeing Lucky's fourteen-year-old lively body sitting on the decrepit, mossy front steps of the cabin, wishing he had been given the opportunity to spend the summer within the oppressive confines of Flint Ridge rather than within the confines of a child-sized casket.

Before reaching the bunker in which I would have to spend my final summer as a minor, we stopped in front of the middle cabin, which looked more condemned than the others. Mr. Desmond pointed at the dilapidated structure, which I had assumed was used as a lawn machinery repair shop, tool shed, or local dump. To my chagrin, he indicated that it was actually the dining hall where we could get two meals per day, promptly at 10:30 and 3:00. Unfortunately, he meant 10:30 p.m. and 3:00 a.m.; the obscure meal hours instilled a nagging feeling that the days would be long and arduous. He explained that due to cutbacks and a resourceful budgeting scheme, the administrators were able to sway the regulatory board to buying into the inhumane theory that serving two fifteen hundred calorie meals separated by a five-hour block would provide boys with enough sustenance and energy to carry us through each day without negative physiological consequences caused by malnutrition. Once again, I did not challenge or even question the director's financially driven, especially unethical theory, and nodded politely as it had been proven as an effective way of avoiding unwarranted child abuse.

We neared Bunker Eight where Mr. Desmond and his equally barbaric henchman were about to leave me under the supervision of my bunker Counselor, Counselor Arnold. Amused by Mr. Desmond's futile attempt at making Flint Ridge appear to adopt customs similar to that of a whimsical summer camp, I made the mistake of unknowingly rolling my eyes upon hearing the use of the term "Counselor." Acting as though the director and guard needed a team-building exercise, they both seized the opportunity by ganging up on me. Still shackled by my wrists and ankles, I must say it was probably the most one-sided fight in history, yet they still didn't hold back as Mr. Desmond connected with the center of my chest with full force, so much so that I could feel his gaudy gold wedding ring leave an imprint on my sternum. As quickly as the camp director could knock the wind out of my lungs, the sadistically quick-reacting guard swiped my legs from beneath me with a perfectly executed karate kick to the back of my knees with these steel-toed work boots.

"You're a slow learner, aren't you boy?" The guard said as he literally added insult to injury.

Mr. Desmond then chimed in with a supporting, "Oh he will learn. If it's the last thing he does."

Laying on my back in the tall grass, feeling clusters of weeds pierce through various parts of my shirt, I tried to find a breath before my brain shut down due to a lack of oxygen. Feeling as though a dent in my chest needed to be plunged out using a tool from an auto body repair shop, I closed my eyes and focus on catching my breath. Once I regulated my breathing, I pretended like I was trying to gasp for air so as to buy myself a few extra minutes without intervention from my enthusiastically aggressive chaperones. Keeping my eyes closed to ignore the gawking stares of Mr. Desmond and the nameless guard, the many afflictions on my body were aching at different intensities, but all very much present. The pain had brought about a morbid, yet familiar sense of comfort, reminiscent of how I became accustomed to daily lashings back at Aunt Eleanor's house. At that moment, I became wistful of the home I never truly considered to be my home until that day, longing for Perry to lay his hands on me instead of those two power-crazed strangers. Finally experiencing a typical childhood reaction to being away at summer camp, I simply missed my parents and wanted to go home.

 Growing impatient from my delayed ability to rise to my feet, Mr. Desmond disregarded my blatant need for a time-out and grabbed me by the scruff of my neck, bringing me to my feet with one fluid motion. It surprised me how strong Mr. Desmond was and how his presentable attire camouflaged his sheer strength, or at least created the illusion that he subscribed to an elitist status incapable of engaging in physical violence. As I have learned over my particularly long life, a person, despite his or her appearance, can take you by surprise in the most unexpected of ways.

 Once I could stand with minimal assistance from Mr. Desmond and his guard, acting as retaliatory crutches guiding me to Bunker Eight, I was left on the collapsed front porch and was instructed without sympathy,

"Report to Counselor Arnold for a cot assignment and work duty placement immediately."

Exhausted by the physical trauma I had just endured, I had to lean against a termite-ravaged beam upon hearing of my expectation to provide manual labor in my ailing condition. As I tried to recover at an impossibly expedited speed for a human, I braced myself for Counselor Arnold to pick up where Mr. Desmond had left off. I was certain that aggression had been a required trait sought out during the Flint Ridge staff recruitment process.

With their backs turned and beginning to walk away, I stood facing them as I observed the camp from a vantage point higher than before. Although it symbolized imprisonment and punishment for a crime I had committed, it was nevertheless breathtaking. I almost resented the beautiful scenery for creating the illusion of freedom when all I could do was admire it and fantasize about freely walking through the robust trees, perhaps choosing to dip my toes in the brisk water of the nearby creek. It is interesting how paradise could be experienced differently based on circumstances. As an underpaid housekeeper would at a five-star Caribbean resort, I believed that even though I was in a privileged location, I could not enjoy it or bask in the beauty as much as if I had been born under more favorable circumstances. I thought to myself that it was a waste to utilize such pristine space to build a camp that would instill negative feelings in its visitors and imagined how much more respectful it would have been to relocate the camp to an industrial area away from the majestic wilderness. Part of me felt like I didn't deserve to witness the glory of the natural landscape.

While I was struggling with my appreciation for my surroundings and whether I was deserving of such majesty, I was met from behind by a person who had to be Counselor Arnold.

"Welcome, son." Counselor Arnold said in an unexpected tone.

At first hearing a lilting voice, I was taken by surprise as I couldn't believe a woman was employed to supervise a cabin of criminally deviant teenage boys. Greeting me in a soft-spoken, entirely passive voice, I jumped to a reassuring conclusion by sighing with relief that my bunker Counselor was unlike her male colleagues and was uninterested in inflicting pain on me. As I eagerly turned around to introduce myself to the refreshingly pleasant lady, I embarrassingly became startled as I caught a glimpse of the stubble on Counselor Arnold's cleft chin.

Despite my many narrow-minded guardians, ignorant homogenous community, and terrifyingly hateful school administration, I had always carried with me an innate sense of acceptance. This acceptance had been inexplicably instilled as a prideful value since I could remember, which is why I was beside myself in humiliation following my disrespectful reaction to Counselor Arnold's appearance.

"Sorry ma'am," I said as I turned bright red.

Happily excusing my own behavior due to an unfortunate inconsistency between my senses, I hoped my new bunker Counselor did not notice my shocked expression- or at least took little offense to my poor reaction. Trying to scurry past my inopportune reflex, I stuttered as I introduced myself,

"I'm Hunter. N-n-nice to meet you."

I felt my cheeks heat up in a shamefully revealing manner upon shaking Counselor Arnold's intimidatingly firm hand. Regardless of the Counselor's initial affable demeanor, I was unwilling to partake in any additional assumptions in case there was a ruthless temper hidden behind his deceivingly calming voice.

"Nice to meet you, Hunter. I'm Counselor Arnold and I'll be looking after you this summer." Arnold said with out-of-place authenticity.

As we continued to speak with one another, it became quickly apparent that Counselor Arnold meant no harm to me and took his role of bunker Counselor seriously, choosing to focus on rehabilitation and structure rather than reactive corporal punishment. Arnold sincerely told me,

"Being entrusted with the supervision of the older boys at Flint Ridge was a job I don't take lightly. And, unlike my colleagues, I rely on compassion as much as I do discipline. How does that sound, Hunter?"

I responded with a relieved yet skeptical, "Sounds good."

Inviting me into Bunker Eight, Arnold opened the rickety screen door and gestured for me to go ahead. Walking into the cabin lit only by sunlight peering in through the far dusty window at the back of the bunker, I was sickened by the smell of the stagnant air. It was beyond me how the freshest, most unpolluted country air my lungs have ever had the pleasure of breathing could transform into smelling like what could only be described as a sweaty gym sock floating in a bucket of old deep fryer oil.

Due to a cabin full of unhygienic adolescent boys, I longed for the odor of my old locker room and feared having to sleep surrounded by such dizzying aromas. The fact is that I was far from prissy or even critical regarding the types of distasteful environments I frequented, but this particular cabin had pushed the boundaries of my agreeableness. Sadly, by the end of the summer, I became so acclimated to the various revolting scents that I would not be able to identify the putrid essence of Bunker Eight. Humbly stated, there is no doubt that I would soon contribute to the detestable air quality. Even Counselor Arnold seemed to be unaffected by the nauseating smell.

"You'll get used to that funk. Mold and B.O. if you were wondering," Arnold said in amusement with my disgusted expression.

Once again being misled by my differing senses, I was astonished to see how organized and proper the inside of the cabin was maintained. Reinforced by Counselor Arnold's strict instructions regarding his expectation of keeping a neatly made, military-style bed and proper storage of personal items in each assigned foot locker, there had been a respectful standard adhered to by all campers.

I walked down the center of the cabin, passing five rows of evenly spaced bunk beds on each side of the room, allowing for accommodations for a maximum of twenty boys at any given time. Offering assistance on how to properly make up a bed, Counselor Arnold stated that his years in the military gave him the necessary knowledge to tuck the sheets so tightly that his own sleeping quarters could act as a trampoline. Believing his attention to detail from the twenty identical beds, each covered with a white sheet, beige wool blanket, and slender pillow tucked in a white case as if it was being swaddled, I realized I would not be able to get away with an unmade bed as I did with Aunt Eleanor. Granted, I was never given so much as a pillow or an extra blanket at night to reach a basic level of comfort, but I was certain it was easier than it looked.

Making our way down the buckling floorboards of the drab cabin, we reached the last row of bunk beds, where Counselor Arnold gestured to the bed on the bottom left.

"That's your bunk and your responsibility, Hunter," Arnold said sternly.

Ready for my arrival, there was a collection of toiletries, including a black washcloth, a black toothbrush with an enormous tube of what I assumed what toothpaste despite the appearance similar to that of a tube of caulking, and a yellowish bar of soap the size of a brick. I was instructed to keep track of these items as they were expected to last until the end of my stay and wouldn't be given any replacements. Thinking about the unescapable smell, I jumped to the conclusion that the soap wouldn't last as long as was intended. Hoping to take a load off, relieving the dizziness resulting from an unexpected backward summersault to the ground, I bent down to sit on the bed.

"Don't get too comfortable, Hunter," Arnold explained, "You won't be spending much time relaxing today…or any other day for that matter."

The next welcome gift I received was a pair of black garden work gloves strapped with velcro to a make-shift axe manufactured from a dull square slab of metal atop a piece of splintered plywood. Counselor Arnold handed the tool to me and politely ordered me out the cabin door to meet the rest of the campers for work duty. Walking ahead of me as I followed closely, I got the chance to discretely observe Counselor Arnold without being mistaken as rude or intrusive. I fear I failed to not stare in a discriminatory manner and worried I'd be caught in the act as I induced a gender based on physical attributes. From what I could observe in the seconds it took us to reach the door, Counselor Arnold was quite tall, nearly half a foot taller than myself, and slender in most areas a man would carry some bulk. However, I noticed his calves, triceps, and deltoids sculpted in a fashion typical of either an athletic man or woman. Based on my limited knowledge of anatomy and gender-specific attributes, I could not make an educated decision regarding which pronoun to use when referring to Counselor Arnold.

At the time, the world had created an obsession surrounding labels attributed to sexual orientation, gender, race, and religion, making it quite unsettling to address people by their preferred identity. The number of distinguishing labels that existed to describe a variety of cultures, subcultures, and minority groups grew so fast that it was easy to mistakenly refer to an individual or group by an outdated or inaccurate identifier. Consequently, I refrained from even attempting to correctly identify ambiguous individuals on the basis that I feared both insulting the person and appearing ignorant.

With that in mind, I was ready to steer clear of pronouns and specific identifiers for the remainder of the summer just to avoid engaging in an awkward conversation. Satisfied with my decision to avoid the issue rather than simply ask Counselor Arnold what gender he identified as at the expense of sounding rude, I couldn't help but try to figure it out for myself before letting it go. Since it was right in front of me, my eyes became glued to his backside, noticing that specific area to be particularly substantial, an ambiguous trait that again could indicate being athletic or in fact a biological woman. Preoccupied with my inner debate, I forgot to avert my inappropriate stare, allowing me to get caught ogling my bunker Counselor's rear end.

Uninhibitedly addressing my inappropriate gaze, Counselor Arnold said in an uncharacteristically angry voice,

"Hunter! Look me in the eyes and show me the respect I deserve."

I replied in fear and mumbled, "Sorry ma'am…I mean, sir."

From my beet-red face and inability to maintain eye contact, Arnold knew that I meant no disrespect, rather succumbing to an innocent form of curiosity. Perhaps his initial outrage was due to the fact that he was also embarrassed because he became less defensive once I tried to physically remove myself from the awkwardness, tripping down the broken front porch steps. Counselor Arnold called me back before I could get too far, realizing that I had only one question on my mind, and reassured me by saying in a comforting tone,

"Don't worry, Hunter. I get it. You're not alone, most people experience some varying level of discomfort when they first meet me."

To which I replied, "Sure, but I still didn't mean anything by it."

"I know. I can tell you're a good egg." Arnold said as he tried to hide a slight smirk.

He then calmly and confidently explained that he was a biological male but was in the process of making the transformation to his true self and preferred the "she/her" pronouns. Using what could have been taken as a degrading incident instead as an opportunity to educate me on her experience as a transgendered person and the gender dysphoria she had felt for much of her life, I was advised to simply ask in the future if I needed further clarification as she was proud to share more about her identity. Having met the first rational adult in my entire life, I was both confused and in awe with how frank Counselor Arnold was and how she could speak to me as respectfully as she would another adult. It was an unfamiliar and odd feeling to be spoken to without hostility and disdain, leading me to believe that there was a much more enjoyable dynamic to be shared with my elders.

Once the "Full House-esque" heartwarmingly educational moment was over and I had been given the knowledge I needed to approach similar situations in the future, the dynamic shifted back from teacher-student to Counselor-camper. Requesting that I follow her again, Counselor Arnold led me behind Bunker Eight toward the ridge at the top of the hill. With my gloves and axe in hand, I kept up with her despite the lethargy resulting from my ailing body. Noticing that I was struggling to keep up with her, not to mention having difficulty keeping a pace indicative of a sober person, she finally inquired about the gash on my nose,

    "Do you need a bandage or some ice?"

    "No, I'm good. Thanks." I responded with a hardened façade.

    "Tough guy, eh?" She said in an intensely deep voice.

I continued to refuse her offer to avoid any inference that I was not invincible, to which she saw right through and took it upon herself to place a plastic bandage on the bridge of my nose to stop the bleeding. After making sure it was on tight, she acknowledged her boss' uneven temperament and apologized for the unnecessary punishment, adding that she did not understand how intimidation could be interpreted as an effective form of discipline. Unsure as to what she meant, seeing as how my seventeen years on Earth had been shaped by that mere philosophy, I simply nodded skeptically and failed to consider other potential forms of discipline.

    We continued on our way up the inclined slope that led to the ridge from which the camp was named until we reached the summit after a modest two-hundred-foot trek. Looking over the edge of Flint Ridge, down on the camp below, I had a bird's eye view of the encompassing terrain, allowing me to experience a panoramic view of the wilderness. Surrounded by deep ravines, uniquely shaped towering mountains, and unobstructed rushing streams, it was hard to imagine why a civilization would aspire to alter an already complex and beautiful landscape. Looking even more surreal than before, I wanted to stay perched on that rock for as long as possible, avoiding our destination that involved some sort of manual labor requiring an axe. However, Counselor Arnold stayed true to her aversion to providing me with comfort and told me to come along as she continued walking past the peak of the ridge and down the other side of the hill.

Distracted by the serene environment, I fell so far behind that I could not see which direction Counselor Arnold had taken once she cleared the side of the ridge. Fearing I had tested her patience to the point of abandoning her passive attitude toward discipline, I ran to close the gap between us. As I picked up my speed with difficulty as the sharp incline over the ridge brought me to all fours, I used my hands to pull my body over the protruding rocks. My upper body created too much momentum as I surpassed the ridge, not realizing that there had been a significant drop on the opposing side, propelling my torso down the jagged land at an accelerated speed.

Fortunately, the underestimation of my upper body strength had given me the momentum to catch up with Counselor Arnold. To my dismay, my first introduction to the juvenile delinquents I would associate with for the summer consisted of me bellowing in an effeminate shriek as my flailing body came to a gradual halt at their feet. Too disheartened to appear vulnerable in front of a group of my peers, who had already begun spouting jeers and slanders in response to my cowardly, albeit uncoordinated entrance, I casually lifted myself up and brushed off the dust from my torn sweatpants. Even Counselor Arnold found my entrance to be amusing as she ineffectively masked a single chuckle with a fake cough as she introduced me to the rest of the group.

"Campers, meet Hunter. He'll be helping us out this summer, so treat him with the same respect you treat me. Got it?"

Arnold shouted to the group.

The group responded in a united, well-rehearsed chant, "Yes, Counselor Arnold!"

Following my brief introduction, I was instructed that the work detail was to clear the entire twenty acres of thriving forest by summer's end in anticipation of a new development being built. Having to uncomfortably slant my neck at an unnatural angle, I took a step back to see the tops of the mighty trees. Even the pine and spruce trees appeared to tower over the ridge behind me, dwarfed by the breathtakingly enormous Sequoias that rocketed from the rich soil, looking as though they were within inches of piercing the descending clouds above. Nearly feeling claustrophobic from the monstrous plants creating a canopy over my head, but also creating a shelter by shielding my head from the scalding summer sun, I felt like I was back in my old neighborhood. I imagined feeling the draft of the shadows cast by the sun-blocking thirty-story subsidized housing buildings. Intimidated by the magnificent size of the ancestral trees, I had little faith in my ability to pierce the tree's thick bark, let alone get far enough through the trunk for it to topple over. It seemed like a job fit for a muscular lumberjack, not an unathletic, city-dwelling seventeen-year-old.

Being that it was the beginning of summer, not much of the forest had been cleared by the rest of the higher seniority Flint Ridge campers, meaning we had our work cut out for us. Noticing that by the time I slid into the work site, many of the trees my fellow inmates had been working on were about halfway chopped. It was apparent that I had to catch up. Disregarding the ridicule from the odd boy as I walked over to the edge of the tree line, I found an available pine tree away from the rest of the group. Keeping my eyes focused on the tree trunk, I started swinging the axe with full force in an attempt to make up for lost time.

    Being from the city, I had never cut down a tree before, not even around Christmas, but I figured the logistics were simple enough and continued to hack away at an ambitious rate. The harder I swung, the more attention I directed towards myself, noticing from the corner of my eye that the nearest boy stopped his own chopping to watch me in disbelief. Realizing that the one boy's interest in my work with the tree developed into several overseers, I picked up the pace and rapidly started hitting the tree until sweat collected on the fuzz of my upper lip. Holding onto the axe so tightly, I could feel the thin burlap on the gloves begin to tear, exposing my fingertips and palms of my hands to the piercing splinters of the slightly cracked axe handle. I once again pushed through the pain and disregarded the blisters that immediately began to form all over my already callused hands.

    Flattered by the attention I was receiving from the originally unimpressed group of boys, every one of them had stopped what they were doing to observe my newfound lumberjack skills. Basking in the attention received for a skill I didn't even know I had until picking up the axe, I hoped the tree would soon crack. Although I wouldn't let my spectators notice my discomfort, my arms were beginning to burn and my hands were becoming numb from the constant vibrations from the metal banging into the solid trunk over and over. Despite my increasingly powerful repetitions, the mighty pine would not budge. However much I wanted to persevere and show those seasoned manual laborers that a city boy could just as easily get the job done, there wasn't any strength left in my arms. My forearms and hands had seized up, leaving me utterly useless in the face of the unwavering tree. Drenched in sweat, and sporting torn gloves streaked with my own stubborn blood, I dropped the axe to the ground and bravely turned to gauge the reaction from the crowd behind me - even Counselor Arnold had been watching in amazement. As my face met theirs, I was instantly taunted as the ignorant city slicker they all pegged me to be.

"First time using an axe, city boy?" One boy exclaimed in laughter.

Apparently, I had been using the blunt side of the axe, which is why I had so much trouble with the seemingly dull blade. As one of the more obnoxious boys came forward to both patronize me and point out the difference between the dull and sharp sides of an axe, he looked back to rile up the audience of onlookers.

"We've got a genius here, boys!" The boy shouted in amusement.

Another boy joined the ridicule and said, "At least we know he's not here 'cause he's an axe murderer!"

As the cackles and insults poured from the unforgiving crowd of confident teenage boys, I had surpassed my limit for abuse that day and reverted to the ways of my neighborhood to release some pent-up aggression. Before Counselor Arnold could stop what he had perceived to be an imminent threat towards one of his campers, I picked up the axe that had facilitated my humiliation by the handle with both hands and swung the blunt instrument at the right side of the obnoxiously taunting boy's head, who was dangerously standing with his back to me. Perhaps I didn't know how to use an axe properly or conduct myself befitting a rural environment, but I would say not turning your back on someone you had just publicly humiliated was common sense in the city.

"That's how you use an axe, asshole!" I said enraged.

Briefly proud of my attack on the attention-starved boy, I realized the action might have been short-sighted when the crowd of enraged delinquents banded together and retaliated. Before Counselor Arnold could intervene and bring me to a safe place to be disciplined properly, I was incapacitated by nearly twenty teenage boys, all of whom had missed a good brawl since being incarcerated at Flint Ridge. Amidst the punching, kicking, elbowing, and all other things brutal, I knew from experience that if I were to curl into a ball and protect both my head and genitalia, I might be able to walk away relatively unscathed. So, I laid down on the ground at the center of a violent dog pile like a scared potato bug until Counselor Arnold was physically able to tear through the relentless group of savages and rescue me.

Eventually, Counselor Arnold did get through the pack of feral campers after about five minutes of effortlessly tossing adrenaline-filled boys off from top of me. Proving to be the most impressive woman I had ever laid eyes on, she grabbed me by the back of the neck with one hand while she fended off the blood-thirsty fighters. Once we were removed from the chaos ensuing down by the wooded area, Counselor Arnold barked an order directly at me,

"Hunter! Get your ass to the top of the ridge and don't move until I get you."

Then, with a ground-trembling roar that sounded like it could have started a devastating rock slide, she threatened the rest of the energized boys,

"All of you, grab your axes and get back to chopping before each of them was sent to "The Pit" for the rest of the day."

Upon mention of "The Pit" every one of the poser anarchists fell in line and quickly returned to cutting down their respective trees to avoid spending any time whatsoever in "The Pit". As Counselor Arnold went to inspect the injury inflicted on the boy still lying unconscious on the ground, I wondered what "The Pit" consisted of and whether it was in fact a real pit or just a frightening name. Regardless of what it actually was, I feared I would soon find out as punishment for my aggressive, albeit provoked, attack with what could be viewed as a deadly weapon.

I looked down at Counselor Arnold assessing the severity of the boy's injuries. First jumping to the worst-case scenario by checking the pulse on the side of his neck, she pressed her two fingers into a stream of blood that was running from his temple. Noticing an expression of relief wash over her face, it was apparent that she did in fact feel a pulse, meaning she wouldn't have to explain a death on her watch and more importantly, I wouldn't be transferred to an adult maximum security penitentiary to serve a life sentence as an adult. Equally relieved that the boy was still alive, I waited in horror as Counselor Arnold slowly brought him back to consciousness. Next, I could see that the boy was asked to count the number of fingers she was holding up; I became concerned as he was asked again, indicating a wrong answer and impaired mental functioning. I wish I could say my main concern was the annoying boy's well-being, but truth be told, I could not bear the guilt of having another young boy's death on my conscience.

As I waited on pins and needles for any indication that I hadn't wasted another life, I could see the boy snap out of the mental fog I had thrust upon him as Counselor Arnold helped him shake off his imbalance to regain equilibrium. I thanked the manifesting stars above for redemption in the face of yet another misguided, impulsive action and welcomed my impending punishment in the unanimously feared "pit." Seeming as though there was in fact no rest for the wicked, the dazed boy was handed his axe and faced toward the tree he had been chopping before I made a spectacle out of myself. I could hear Counselor Arnold as she made her way back up the ridge, promising the group of minor lumberjacks that they would finish their quota regardless of the excitement of the evening and to be careful of where they swung their axes in the dark.

When I locked eyes with Counselor Arnold, I didn't need her to give me directions as to where I was expected to walk, I simply reacted to the intensity in her eyes and started walking down the opposite side of the ridge back toward the cabin. The short walk back down to the grassy area was spent in complete hostile and resentful quietness until we reached the rear of Bunker Eight. Expecting I would be given a lecture on either safety or impulse control, I naïvely kept walking towards the porch of the cabin where I assumed a mandated discussion would take place. To my apprehension and utter surprise, Counselor Arnold waived the need to discuss the consequences of my harmful actions and merely cleared her throat to signal me to stop and hastily return to her position. Without saying a word, she veered to the right and walked behind the bunker with me trailing as an insecure shadow, passing both the dining hall and Bunker Seven. Dusk had consumed the sky right before my very eyes, leaving little time to adjust to the enclosing darkness falling from the rural night sky, impairing my vision of what lay ahead of me.

    Still adhering to a strict vow of silence, Counselor Arnold said more with her grunts and scolding stare than she could have articulated with the most eloquently stated words. She then led me to what looked like a manhole cover and pried it open using a long steel pole that had been left next to a nearby shrub. Once the heavy cover was removed, Counselor Arnold welcomed me to "The Pit" by stating,

    "I am not an advocate of solitary confinement in an unsafe enclosure, and especially for adolescents, but extreme cases require extreme corrective measures."

I walked to the open perimeter of the hole, trying to blindly measure the depth of The Pit before agreeing to enter it. As I bent down to get a closer look at the worrisome hole, Counselor Arnold positioned herself in a crouched position, suggesting that I bend my legs to avoid breaking a bone. She then proceeded to swiftly nudge me forward.

My heart skipped an essential beat as I was pushed down The Pit with little warning, falling for an unknown distance or amount of time. However long it took me to hit the bottom, it was apparent that I was able to lose my breath at least once on the way down. Remembering Counselor Arnold's sage advice, I bent my knees before hitting the bedrock below, which indeed softened the impact on my brittle bones. Disoriented by the tumble down an abyss, I waved my hands around the narrow, vertical tunnel in hopes of finding a hole in the slippery stoned wall to grip and climb out. Unable to feel anything but broken roots and moist soil, I hadn't the slightest idea as to how I would eventually free myself from the depths of that impromptu dungeon. In response to the audible hyperventilation and frantic stirring at the bottom of The Pit, I could hear Counselor Arnold speaking from above,

"All right down there, Hunter?" Then continuing to speak before I could give an answer she didn't want ot hear. "Good. Sit tight and I'll come get you before bed checks. But don't worry, I'll cover the hole so that no critters fall down there with you."

Unaware how long I would be stuck several feet below the ground, since I did not know when the beds were routinely checked, I considered myself to be doomed. I then wondered why they didn't kill two birds with one stone by throwing me down in a coffin to save themselves some trouble in the long run. Realizing that I may have been made aware of two fears following an inconsiderate push into that forsaken pit, it was apparent that I wasn't a fan of both heights and confined spaces. With the manhole cover blocking out the moon's hypnotizing glow, I was left in the pitch-black darkness;

an environment better suiting a burrowing rodent or slithering earthworm. Left without any sort of timepiece to track the time with an accurate understanding of when I was expected to be freed, I had no bearing on the amount of time that had elapsed since being at the bottom of what I deemed to be a dried-up old well.

Ironically trying to look on the bright side while stranded at the bottom of the infamous pit, I suspected I was safer in complete solitude than confined to a cabin occupied by my newest enemies. I did not blame them for reacting as defensively as they did, since I would have done the same for a friend or neighborhood kid in need. As much as I empathized with the group of hot-tempered boys, I knew it wouldn't be worth my labored breath to explain myself as I too wouldn't be quick to offer forgiveness following such a memorable brawl. My hope was that either someone or something exceedingly noteworthy would distract them by the time I returned, allowing me to sufficiently integrate myself into the social group, and as a result, avoid daily beatings from my bunkmates.

As hard as I tried to imagine a scenario where I'd return to Bunker Eight and receive a warm welcome from forgiving and compassionate campers, I remembered that Flint Ridge was not a typical camp with run-of-the-mill campers. Instead, I braced myself with reality and expected the worst while I sat back against the exposed wet soil, closing my eyes for the first time in what felt like weeks. My eyelids burned once I finally let them rest, realizing the strain from keeping them open for what felt like months. Perhaps it was still guilt or it was paranoia that my life was at risk for allowing Lucky's to be taken in cold blood, but I was kept awake every night since. Just as I feared, once my eyelids closed, even though it didn't increase the level of darkness, I instantly saw Lucky's youthful face lying dead on Richler Street with an undeserved bullet in the back of his head. What angered me and made me feel even more remorseful was why Stan's poor aim inadvertently struck Lucky instead of me, who had been the one wielding the gun. While Lucky's death didn't make a lick of sense to me, my survival is what disturbed me most of all.

I opened my eyes once I realized that every time they shut, it triggered my mind to press play on the short film about Lucky's untimely death. Stuck on repeat, like an irritating three-second GIF, my brain was hell-bent on torturing me with the vividly gruesome image of my young friend's morbidly lifeless body. I was left to my own twisted devices for what felt like an eternity; I became weary of Counselor Arnold's intention to return for me at all.

My intensifying paranoia led me to consider the possibility that she may have forgotten where The Pit was located in the disorienting darkness of night or perhaps Mr. Desmond had instructed her to leave me to eventually decompose as a convenient way to get rid of me. For a moment, I wished my paranoid thoughts were justified in reality, realizing that I was in the safest place I could be, protected from abusive guardians and peers alike. Not only was I liberated from the unfair treatment of others, but I was also virtually unable to cause any more harm to myself or others. It appeared that freedom was not a flattering attribute.

5

I had given up hope at some point during the countless hours I spent at the bottom of The Pit, finally accepting a life abandoned underground. Then, as my future as a surfaced-dweller seemed to be lost, I rejoiced as I heard the heavy manhole being pried open, then hearing the thud of the steel impacting the ground above. Although I still couldn't see anything, I could once again hear Counselor Arnold shouting from above,

"All right, Hunter. You're done. Stand up and grab my hand."

Doing as I was told, I pushed my back against the cold wall and propped myself to my feet. Standing tall, I awkwardly realized that the opening of The Pit had only been about a foot and a half over my head. Feeling defeated by my own dramatic perception of the relatively short fall to the floor of the seven-foot-deep pit, I was again misled by my exaggerated senses when Counselor Arnold apologized for leaving me down there for so long, explaining that she had to deal with a mishap and lost track of time; before she knew it, a half an hour had passed.

Coming to terms with the fact that I had not been trapped in a dried-up well all night, and was basically sitting in a rabbit hole for thirty minutes, I let Counselor Arnold pull me out from the depths of my own insanity. She then began lecturing me about how seriously I could have hurt Finn. Noting that my rage and disregard for consequences would lead me into a world of trouble, one filled with prison bars and life sentences. She assured me that she had seen many boys my age with more self-control get lost down a path they could not easily backtrack. Trying to appeal to the fact that I did not see myself as a lost cause with an irreversible criminal record and inevitably bleak future, she made me acknowledge what she was saying by forcing me to repeat a mantra she had optimistically created: "Foresight yields hope."

Finding her vague, cliché motivational mantra to have no bearing on my own circumstances, I humored her to appear cooperative. Satisfied with my unenthusiastic repetition of her existentially shallow slogan, Counselor Arnold led me back to Bunker Eight to get reacquainted with the rest of the campers. Walking around the side of the cabin, there was a line of axes wedged in the horizontal log beams with the blades stuck deep in the solid wood. On the handles of the axes, various-sized gloves were hanging from the ends to identify which axe belonged to each camper. I noticed my axe at the end of the row by the tattered, blood-stained gloves hanging by a torn velcro loop. I guess I hadn't done a bad enough job at chopping down trees to warrant a change in work detail, as I would have hoped.

Calling it a day, Counselor Arnold left me at Bunker Eight before retiring to her own bed at the administrative building and watched as I showed myself in.

"Be quiet, everyone is sleeping and you waking them up is the last thing anyone needs at this hour. I don't need another riot on my hands," she said determined to sleep off an eventful day.

Agreeing that calling attention to myself would not be in my interest,

I slowly opened the rickety screen door, then gently guided it back towards the door frame, holding it close to my body like I was taking the lead in a romantic dance. Once the door was closed without so much as a squeak from the rusted hinges, I removed my mud-caked sneakers and lifted myself on the tips of my toes in hopes that my wet socks would act as a silencer between my feet and the noisy floor boards. Except for one or two faint creaks, I made it all the way to the end of the row of bunk beds without waking a single one of the sleeping delinquents in the cabin.

Despite my insomnia, I was very much ready to rest my head on something more welcoming than a wall of dirt. Even though I didn't expect the pillow that had been provided to me to be particularly soft, I counted myself as lucky to actually have one at night. I eased myself onto the bed without arousing my bunkmate up above and carefully undressed, in part to avoid making noise but primarily because my entire body hurt in one way or another. Once I removed all my clothing, except for a scratchy pair of government-issued white cotton boxers, I peeled back the wool sheet to climb into the warm bed. Even on the hottest of summer nights, time spent at the bottom of The Pit chilled me to the bone. Excited to slip in between the cozy covers, I first tested the waters of my seemingly standard bed by extending my leg down the middle of the mattress. Before I could straighten my leg, I hooked what felt like a sleek piece of chewed gum covered in saliva. Irked by the unpleasant sensation, I threw the cover to the side to identify what I assumed was the result of shotty housekeeping. Wishing it had in fact been a piece of chewing gum, my bellows of disgust were reciprocated with an uproar of laughter and cheering as I correctly identified it as a used condom.

Realizing that my prior attack on Finn had been retaliated not with violence but with a revolting prank, my devastated reaction satiated the group's need for revenge. Unwilling to climb back into a bed contaminated with that biohazard, I stood vulnerably in my revealing white boxers as I received ridicule from my fellow campers for the third time that day. Coming forward to claim ownership of the prank, Finn, who looked unaffected by the blow to his head, stated facetiously,

"Hey Hunter, I was saving that for one of the girls over at Flint Valley!" then suggested, "But you look lonelier than they do, so have at it."

Taunted by a roar of laughter, Finn was encouraged to pick up the condom and throw it at my face. Reacting to a stunt that would have warranted a severe beating back home, I leaped forward and grabbed Finn by his neck, pinning him up against the pillar of my bunkbed.

The sight of the dastardly prank from the corner of my eye provoked me to tighten the already vice-like grip I had on Finn's neck. To deter the rest of the anxiously hostile company from interfering, I shouted in the air,

"Come any closer and I'll crush his fucking throat!"

Unable to restrain my anger, I could feel myself losing control. The tighter my hand fastened around the boy's scrawny neck, the more red and swollen his face became, until eventually, his eyes started to drift to the back of his head as I cut off his oxygen supply. Undeterred from ending his life right then, the fading look on his panicked face transformed into that of Lucky, startling me into letting go.

As Finn hit the floor, I could see his face as he gasped for a breath of air, focused on inhaling through his mangled throat. Stunned by the confusing hallucination, I sat back down on my bed in time for Counselor Arnold to barge through the cabin door. Responding to the racket caused by the unsanitary prank and subsequent strangulation, she demanded to know what was going on as she could hear the ruckus from the main hall. Rather than rat on me, thereby reserving my accommodations at the bottom of The Pit for the rest of the night, the residents of Bunker Eight withheld information about the condemning events that had just transpired and silently slid back into their respective beds.

Noticing that Finn was lying next to my bunk in distress when he should have been at the front of the cabin at the top of the first row of bunkbeds, Counselor Arnold questioned him,

"Finn. Care to share?"

Although he spoke with difficulty, Finn merely rubbed his throat and lied, saying,

"I was jumping from bed to bed, missed the mattress and hit the frame."

"Hit the frame with your throat?" Counselor Arnold said skeptically.

"Yep." Finn replied quickly.

Perceptive enough to realize he was lying, but too tired to probe any further, Counselor Arnold threatened us by saying,

"Keep this up and you'll all be getting 2:00 a.m. wake-up

call, seeing as how you clearly already had enough sleep for the night."

She then left the cabin in a huff, leaving us behind in silence. That is how the rest of the night was spent: in complete silence. Following that act of comradery, I was shown the first glimpse of mutual respect from my fellow delinquents since arriving at Flint Ridge, instilling a sense of comfort I had known very well on the streets of my old neighborhood.

 Wishing I could have slept that night, I was instead haunted by the vision of Lucky's lifeless face. At the time, I couldn't comprehend why his death had such an impact on me. There had been weekly drive-by shootings and fatal gang wars the very streets I took my first steps. Growing up where I did, the concept of being in the wrong place at the wrong time was at the back of my mind regardless of whatever trivial or fun activity I was engaging in. Even with this readiness to embrace the worst at even the most unanticipated times, Lucky dying from a gunshot just seemed too dramatic to believe or even accept. I also wondered how Lucky's father took the news of his son's death but figured he would've simply stayed in an exceptionally oblivious drunken stupor, preventing him from ever really feeling grief, or any genuine emotion for that matter. Fixated on how Lucky died in vain and the possibility that he would most probably not be remembered in a flattering light by most people in his life, let alone his own father, I wondered if life was as meaningful and precious as we are narcissistically led to believe.

 Spending the entire night lost in morbid existential thought, my attention was abruptly averted in the early hours of the morning when the creaking of the screen door was followed by a shocking slamming sound. Reminding me of the gunshot Stan had fired into unsuspecting Lucky, I panicked at the thought that Finn had found a firearm. I instantly envisioned a scenario where he chose to play possum throughout the night until he was ready to retaliate for bludgeoning, and later choking him. I rolled out from under my sheets, hitting the uneven wooden floor with my elbows before ducking my head under the bunkbed frame. Irrationally hiding under a plywood bed frame from a deadly weapon, I grew suspicious of the lack of alarm from my bunkmates. The rest of Bunker Eight responded to the loud explosion nonchalantly, as if they were all too familiar with the sound. I then peered out from underneath my bed and saw the other boys dragging themselves out of bed in agony, beginning to dress in the sweat-stained clothes they had worn the previous day.

As everyone began filing out of the cabin, I assumed that they were disturbingly desensitized to gun violence at Flint Ridge. Either that or they had just responded to their morning wakeup call. Following their lead despite how odd I found their behavior, I saw Finn struggling to put on his sweatpants with his left eye glued shut in hopes of returning to a state of slumber. Reassured that I hadn't been targeted by a disgruntled juvenile delinquent, I marched out of the cabin into the brisk country morning air. Never before seeing frost in the summertime, I looked at the grass and shrubbery in disbelief like a child on his first white Christmas morning. Coming from the city, I had never been in a position to experience such a seasonal phenomenon as the smog usually kept the city temperature consistently blistering at any hour of any given day. Seeing my breath hang in the frigid June air, I felt as though I had been transported to another country - if not an entirely new planet. Fortunately, I was wearing the only sweatpants I had been given, which provided me with enough warmth to keep my extremities from freezing.

Continuing to follow the rest of Bunker Eight, we walked around the side of the log cabin where each boy retrieved their axe that had been wedged. Once the axe was released from the dew-soaked wood, we unenthusiastically walked single file up and down the ridge to start our daily tree chopping. Upon our arrival, I could see Counselor Arnold anxiously waiting at the perimeter of the tree line for us to gather for her morning motivational speech.

Singling me out, she said jokingly, "Hope my morning firecracker didn't startle ya, Hunter. My alarm clock is on the fritz."

At least my suspicion of a rogue gunman lurking around every tree and bush on Flint Ridge property had been dismissed, but I would have indeed appreciated a heads-up before allowing my mind to jump to such extreme scenarios. Once the exhausted stragglers had caught up with the rest of the group, Counselor Arnold explained,

"With all the commotion yesterday," pointing her axe directly at me, "we are way behind on our weekly quota, which means we need to pick up the pace."

Responding to eyerolls and synchronized grunts, Arnold quipped, "Unless you'd prefer to skip breakfast and lunch?"

Heeding her warning, we all got to work. "Thought so," she said with vindication. "Of course," she continued, "I could always tell Mr. Desmond that you'd prefer a different work detail. Maybe a few days at the sewage processing plant would spark some appreciation."

Even though my stomach was empty, phantom smells of human waste and sewage wafted through the air, overpowering the pleasant fragrance of pine. It was a that moment when I realized things could somehow be worse. Although there was not even a sewage processing plant in sight, even from the peak of Flint Ridge, the campers responded to the seemingly substantiated threat and began chopping into the first staggered row of trees.

Walking toward the pine tree I failed to cut down with the blunt edge of the axe, the bark was barely pierced by my many swings. This time, rotating the axe with the blade facing the tree trunk, I lifted the heavy tool to the side of my head and let the momentum of the weight swing the axe into the tree. With less effort than previously utilized, the art of tree chopping was much more enjoyable than I had been led to believe. Making admirable progress, I was hacking through the sap-drenched wood as quickly, if not at a faster pace, than the other, more experienced campers. That said, I was sure to look over several times to make sure I was cutting the trunk in the right place to avoid another reason to bring negative attention upon myself. After about fifteen minutes of chopping, already covered in chunks of bark stuck to me with the natural adhesive oozing from the pine, I had created a wedge two-thirds into the diameter of the trunk. Following one last well-executed swoop, the blade of my axe made contact with the once sturdy tree and started to lean backward. As the remaining piece of tree trunk cracked, the top-heavy pine fell towards the crowded forest, hitting another tree on its way down. Upon collision, the mighty pine cracked the trunk of another resting behind it, cracking its trunk on its way down.

As the first tree I had ever attempted to cut down was laying at a forty-five-degree angle, being supported by the tree that had gotten in its way, it appeared I had gotten myself in quite the predicament. The second tree had been bearing the weight of the first, so Counselor Arnold walked up to inspect the situation, rightfully not willing to trust an amateur like myself to properly approach the natural quandary. She then walked over to the tree supporting the weight of the first and tried with all of her might to budge the heavy tree. Unsuccessful, she tried her luck with the leaning tree, pushing on the trunk like she was Sisyphus rolling a boulder up a hill. Confused as to what would effectively lower the two trees without standing in a compromised position, Counselor Arnold took the axe from my hands and walked over to the base of the second tree. She ran her fingers along the ridges of the untouched bark, as if she was trying to find a sweet spot, then raised the axe above her head like she was about to drive a golf ball three hundred meters and swung into the tree. Hitting the trunk with such velocity, the axe swung right through the trunk and came right out the other side. The supporting tree swiftly fell to the ground, thereby allowing my tree to break free. Visibly impressed by her own accuracy with an axe, Counselor Arnold swung it over her shoulder like a

Buckingham Palace guard before tossing it back into my hands.

Witnessing an astonishing combination of sheer power and precise strategy, I was truly in awe. Ready to take on my next tree, hoping it wouldn't result in the same sort of forestry puzzle for Counselor Arnold to solve, I ventured deep into the woods. Soon, I stood before a Giant Redwood that would surely test my strength and stamina. Chopping through this behemoth would undoubtedly show Counselor Arnold just how strong I am.

Unlike the two pines, this tree was more massive than any tree I had ever seen; I needed to take two steps in either direction to just look around the monstrosity. Nevertheless, I accepted the challenge and imitated Counselor Arnold's stance to mimic her impressive swing. Holding the axe over my head like a sword more than a golf club, I had let the heavy tool hang too far behind my head, causing my underdeveloped body to sway backward as my feet shuffled in the same direction. Expecting my body to fall directly on the axe behind me, I panicked and without thinking and threw the axe as hard as I could before landing on the ground.

As my gaze was directed up at the clouds floating above, I could hear the axe miraculously making contact with the tree in front of me. Relieved that the stray axe didn't veer off to the side and slice into a camper's back, I exhaled and considered myself lucky. I also assured myself that I wouldn't again try to match the skill of Counselor Arnold until I had a few more fallen trees under my belt. Following the satisfying thud of my axe penetrating the trunk of the Sequoia, I heard a subsequent crack that indicated I had too found the sweet spot of the tree. Still laying on my back, I basked in the random success of cutting down a tree with one random throw. As my ego inflated and I considered a professional career as a lumberjack, I could hear a boy's voice from behind me scream, "Timber!"

Fearfully realizing that it had not been my tree that had been cracking at the trunk, I quickly rolled to the side and covered my head as if I was playing dead. The shadow of an equally large Sequoia (one that had realistically taken the boy behind me all night and day to cut down, rather than one lucky chop from a flying axe) passed over my spinning field of vision. It then hit the ground next to me, leaving an indent on the forest floor where I had unwittingly been laying. I had been laying so close that my face was covered with white debris from the parachute seeds of dying dandelions. Unable to gauge my proximity to the enormous tree, Counselor Arnold came running towards me, muttering prayers to an array of deities in hopes that I had not been crushed. When she verified that I was safe, the hopeful prayers turned into blasphemous slanders, commenting on the obscene number of near-death experiences I had been involved in since my arrival less than twenty-four hours earlier.

"Goddammit, Hunter! Do you have a death wish?!" She belted while trying to catch her breath.

I needn't be reminded of my luck, or more accurately, misfortune, when it came to toying with life and death situations. So, I was relieved when Counselor Arnold wiped the terror-induced perspiration from beneath her black Flint Ridge staff baseball cap and urged us to make our way down to the dining hall for lunch while she composed herself.

Following the lead of my hungry co-workers, I brushed the dandelion seeds off my face and carried my axe down to the dining hall. With a strong reminder from my stomach, I realized that I hadn't eaten even a morsel of food since arriving at Flint Ridge. Of course, hunger pangs were a familiar feeling as I hardly ate back home. Usually, I'd wait until I received a free bagged lunch at school rather than tussle with Perry for whatever junk food he and Eleanor kept locked in the cupboards. Perhaps due to the strenuous physical activity and consistently tiring altercations, I felt starved. I looked forward to whatever fifteen-hundred-calorie meal the kitchen staff had prepared for us that day. It appeared that my stomach had taken control over my feet as well as I had been walking up the ridge at a pace much faster than the others. Unbeknownst to me, their slow pace was indicative of their familiarity with Flint Ridge's cafeteria menu.

Arriving first in line at the dining hall, I waited for the kitchen staff to retract the large metal gate that was securely locked atop the serving counter. Looking at the caged clock behind the counter, it was already 3:35, meaning that the staff was five minutes behind the supposedly prompt schedule. Aggravated by my hunger, I hypocritically judged them for not being punctual enough to respect the physiological needs of growing boys. I hadn't been on time for anything of importance in my life, so my perceived right to tediously nit-pick the preparedness of others was just laughable.

Since they were taking their sweet time putting the final touches on the buffet, I decided to peruse the posted weekly menu instead of allowing my watering mouth to be surprised with the dish of the day. I intently read the paper menu posted on the log wall with two pieces of cheap tape as if I was assessing a complex financial statement or trying to comprehend a verse of Shakespeare.

    Starting with that day, the list was as follows. Monday's meal plan was baked beans and boiled hot dogs for breakfast, as well as buttered noodles for supper. Tuesday offered a slightly different option, frozen pizza for breakfast and again buttered noodles for supper. As for Wednesday, hoping for a little variety to get through the mid-week hump, I was disappointed to see a repeat of Monday's meal options. Losing faith in the culinary imagination held by the chefs at Flint Ridge, glancing down to Thursday offered a little more excitement, but stayed on the same simple track, serving grilled cheese and tomato soup for breakfast, but once again returning to the house special of buttered noodles for supper. Hoping to discover a celebratory meal for Friday to show appreciation for a long week worked, I was yet again misled by my naïve hopes and read that we were once again expecting baked beans and hot dogs for breakfast and buttered noodles for supper. Saturday was equally unsavory as the poster showed that we were to start our weekend with chicken noodle soup and crackers for breakfast and the recurring favorite for supper, buttered noodles. To end the week with a bland bang, Sunday's menu was vague and unappetizing as it only had cabbage listed as the meal, not indicating whether it would be a slaw, roll, or added to another more flavorful ingredient; and yes, buttered noodles came in at a total seven out of seven dinners per week.

    Unimpressed by the limited menu items, I dreaded the lack of variety; at least at school, we were given slices of processed meats and cheese, with the occasional store-bought dessert, such as a fudge brownie or chocolate chip cookie for a treat. I guess incarceration fell far below the poverty line in terms of socioeconomic statuses. Despite the uninspired selection, I would have readily eaten a head of raw cabbage just to satiate my hunger pangs. Moving at an irritatingly slow speed behind the counter, an elderly woman shuffled out from a storage area in the kitchen to unlock the gate over the serving counter. Looking familiar, I noticed it was the woman with the chronic cough who had taken the photo for my I.D. badge in the intake office; she had apparently been moonlighting as a cafeteria worker. As much as I respected her employment versatility at Flint Ridge, I suspected the administration could have chosen a staff member with less of a tendency to hack up phlegm while dishing out our baked beans and buttered noodles, as they sounded sensuously displeasing without the viscous topping.

Once the gate had been lifted, I scurried up to the counter, standing directly in front of the woman, now sporting a nametag that indicated her name was Lucille. Waiting impatiently for Lucille to cease her fit of mucus-rattled coughing, I was appreciative that she had not yet put on her gloves, as her bare hand was acting as a basin for the unsanitary bodily fluids spewing from her pursed, wrinkled lips. Wiping her hand on her stained apron, she then proceeded to lift a massive aluminum cover with her clean hand before grabbing a large metal spoon with the contaminated one. Becoming squeamish from the lack of a relatively inexpensive vinyl glove budget at Flint Ridge, Lucille submerged the hand that had been sprayed with lung butter (hopefully not the type butter used to douse the noodles with every evening) into the steaming pile of baked beans and dehydrated, overcooked cut hot dogs. As the dark syrup from the baked beans ran down her fingers, trailing all the way down to her varicose vein wrapping around her wrist like a charm bracelet, then to her sun-spotted elbow, she tossed a mountain of the culinary atrocity on my plate and hacked as she tried to scream for the next boy in line to take the next serving.

    I brought my lunch to the nearest seat at one of two long wooden tables, seemingly made from the same rotting logs that the cabin itself had been constructed. Grabbing a tarnished fork from a single discolored, yellow cup filled to capacity with mismatched utensils, I sat down with my back to the serving counter to avoid being reminded of the unhygienic hand that had made contact with the food on my plate. Dizzied by the overwhelming aroma of burning beans and stale hot dog water, the single slowly rotating fan above the center of the room provided little breathing room in terms of air circulation. As the rest of the campers gathered around me, thankfully focused on the slop in front of them rather than engaging in conversation, my mouth was free to bypass the warning signals being sent from my stomach via my nostrils.

    Taking the fork in my hand as hesitantly as an amateur cardiologist performing his first triple bypass, I scooped the bean/mystery meat medley and took an ill-advised look before ingesting it. Watching the watery brown syrup run over the hardened chunks of syrup that hadn't been cleaned off from a previous boy's meal, I closed my eyes and shoveled the overheated portion of food into my mouth. The over-salted sauce dried out my mouth, prompting me to reach for an imaginary glass of water; now realizing that I had overlooked the tray of opaque plastic cups to the left of Lucille. Unsure as to whether I should start chewing or simply spit it out and go hungry until I tried my hand at the buttered noodles served in five hours, the rumble in my stomach urged me to swallow anything of substance. I started to move my jaw like the pistons of a slow-moving engine, feeling the rubber-like texture of the over-boiled hot dogs bouncing between my molars. As if the chunks of malleable meat weren't bad enough, the beads of mushy beans turned into a grainy, apple sauce-textured substance, losing its structural integrity upon mixing with my saliva. I didn't know how I was supposed to swallow the unholy mixture, let alone finish my plate. The fact that I was expected to eat a meal fit for a swine three times per week for the next thirteen weeks was more of a cruel punishment than an attempt at nourishment.

Having reached my limit for experimental taste-testing, I dropped my fork on the pile of inedible food stuffs and pushed the plate as far away as the narrow table would allow without colliding with a boy's plate on the opposite side. Commenting on my forfeiture, Finn, who had been sitting diagonally from me, unexpectedly said,

"If Lucille caught you throwing out your lunch, you won't get any dinner."

He then graciously offered a tip, "Hold your nose with each bite and imagine it's a juicy bacon cheeseburger."

With that suggestion, I could hear the moans of salivating boys in concert. Opting to taste nothing at all rather than a seasoning that could cure a strip of sirloin steak in a matter of minutes, I followed Finn's instructions and clamped my nose as tightly as I could without opening the gash from the previous day. Noticing that I flinched at the touch of my own fingers, Finn understood that I was not responding to the bad taste in my mouth, but rather to the cut inflicted by the belligerent guard.

He asked, "Did Paul give that to you?" Already knowing the answer before I could speak.

"Depends. Who's Paul?" I asked.

Pointing over to my assailant, Finn said, "Paul is that greasy piece of shit over there."

"Yep, that's him. He didn't seem to like me all that much," I said minimizing the situation.

"He doesn't like anyone. Got messed up from the war, so he doesn't think right." Finn explained as best he could.

a dishonorably discharged soldier whose favorite pass time was inflicting pain on those younger and smaller than himself.

Inciting a common hatred for the power-drunk guard, the rest of the eavesdroppers at the table chimed in with their own stories involving the sadistic authoritative figure. One boy at the far end of the table stated,

"That fat bastard put a cigarette out on my goddam neck!" Failing to whisper as intended, then looking over this shoulder to see if Paul had heard.

"No shit?" I said, concerned.

"Seriously. Then he just lied to Desmond and said that I got stung by a hornet that had flown into the bus. Can you believe that shit?"

The sad part was that I could believe it. Topping each tale with increasingly painful and unthinkable anecdotes, each boy at the table took a turn telling their story of how their stay at Flint Ridge began under the supervision of Paul the guard.

The last and most extreme story was told by a boy about half my already small size, who was sitting directly in front of me. First introducing himself, Jim, or as the other boys referred to him, Slim Jim, an introverted Hispanic boy who hadn't yet experienced a growth spurt, began to speak up.

"I was just minding his own business and looking out the window when Paul accused me of farting," he said with a twisted smile.

Continuing his story, Slim Jum explained that he was confident he did not pass gas in the overreacting guard's presence, so he denied the accusation and continued looking out the window. Infuriated by his perceived insolence and dishonesty, Paul punched poor Slim Jim in the ear so hard that the opposite side of his face collided with the window he had been looking out. Causing the window to crack from the sheer force of the collision with Jim's fragile face, Paul hit him again in the same ear as punishment for the destruction of Flint Ridge property. Although Jim could not hear properly following the blunt blow to his ear, he thinks he heard Paul explain to Mr. Desmond that a crow had flown right into the window at full speed. Laughing at the Director's gullibility, Jim claims that Mr. Desmond accepted the fabrication without suspicion and instead of investigating the bald-faced lie, he commended Paul on keeping the windows so clean that a bird could mistake as open.

As we shared our memories of torment, oddly acting as a refreshing distraction from the offensive meal in front of us, I slowly began to feel like I was bonding with the others. Even Finn, who had seemed to forget about the tension we justifiably should have between us and the understandable hate we could have carried throughout the summer, spoke to me in a manner befitting of a friend. Exchanging ideal ways in which we would give Paul a taste of his own medicine if given the chance, each of us passionately described scenarios where he was incapacitated to one disabled degree or another, making us capable of retaliation. The most creative of vindictive strategies were described in excruciatingly tedious and vivid detail by Jim, who wished,

"I'd tie Paul to the top of one of those big-ass Sequoias, and then chop the fucker down," saying with such enthusiasm.

Getting lost in cruel and unusual punishments involving our nemesis, resident guard and assailant Paul, I had become immersed in a world where we had ultimate control. Such a utopian world would have admittedly been a sound reason for alarm and would most likely require military intervention, but within the bounds of our juvenile minds, it was a world in which we wanted to live. Consumed by fantasies of living carefree lives, free from the wrath of parents and authoritative figures alike, I was lifted to an oblivious state of bliss, unable to foresee an act of initiation about to take place over my shoulder.

As I soon learned, it was Flint Ridge tradition to dump a plate of the day's cafeteria slop over the head of the newcomer. As my lack of luck would have it, I had been the straggler that summer, arriving much later than the rest of the campers due to my lengthy trial being subjected to a string of unnecessary courtroom continuances. Therefore, it was my duty to willingly accept a warm plate of baked beans and hot dogs being poured over my unsuspecting head. Feeling as uncomfortable and unsavory as it did in my mouth, I was forced to sit and bear the laughter of Bunker Eight as bits of hot dog and clumps of sauced beans dripped down my forehead and over my burning red ears.

Initially feeling the rage normally exhibited in response to public humiliation, I wiped the brown sauce from my caked eyes and dislodged a tiny morsel of hot dog from behind my ear. Before I could turn and assault the baked bean bandit, I was overcome with an unexpected giddiness, unable to keep myself from roaring with laughter. Even though I wanted to be angry in the worst way imaginable, I oddly enough found the initiation to be kind of endearing. Laughing uncontrollably, the other boys at my table joined in and laughed with me, most of them reminiscent of their own first day at Flint Ridge. Receiving encouraging slaps on the back and cheers from Finn, who acknowledged my bizarre self-control, I thought to myself that there were definitely worse ways of spending a summer.

Flicking the last bits of stubborn beans and wieners from my shoulders on taunting boys at the table, the fun stopped for a second as the hair on the back of our necks stood up in unison. Hearing the shrill and domineering voice of Paul from outside the dining hall window made us cower in fear of a surprise visit. Listening intently to his shouts bellowing from outside, we were confident that we were safe at the moment as he was directing his demeaning drill sergeant quips at another vulnerable victim.

"Pick up the pace you lazy pieces of shit!" He'd scream.

Taking a quick head count of everyone in the dining hall, we realized that Bunker Eight was filled to capacity and were all in attendance. Curious as to whom Paul had been projecting his inferiority complex, we all rushed to the dusty window facing the administration building and saw Paul unloading a group of scared children onto the Flint Ridge property.

Looking as though the number of children disembarking outnumbered the seats on the short bus, there must have been at least thirty boys much younger than myself. Instructing them with abrupt directions, like a rancher herding cattle into a slaughterhouse pin, Paul established his authority as he put fear into the shaken bunch. As the last child stepped off the bus, joining the others in a straight line in front of the main hall, Mr. Desmond met them like he did the previous day upon my arrival.

We watched uneasily as Mr. Desmond addressed the new arrivals, all waiting for his true character to surface at the drop of a hat, or in that instance, at the sound of a child's laughter. We took pity on the poor child who most likely giggled as a nervous response to the anxiety of being in a strange place, run by intimidating adults. Our hearts clenched as Mr. Desmond promptly responded to the boy's laughter, walked over to the child who must have been no older than twelve years old, and kneed him in the jaw. Connecting with the child's glass jaw, Mr. Desmond's knee had been at the perfect height to easily reach the boy with minimal flexibility. The unexpected blow to the face rendered the young boy unconscious as he flew backward, hitting his head on the side of the bus behind him.

Unable to watch Mr. Desmond and his crony torture defenseless children any longer, we turned away from the single dining hall window and ventured back to our respective seats. Some of the boys hung their heads in shame, while others kicked chairs in anger. Regardless of how each of us reacted, we unanimously resented the unnecessarily brutal way in which Flint Ridge was led. Meanwhile, Lucille no longer felt like dishing out what could in itself be considered a form of torture, because she closed and locked the gate above the serving counter. It was obvious that the new arrivals would have to wait until dinner time to eat.

Interrupting our grief-filled silence, Counselor Arnold barged into the dining hall sarcastically stating,

"Luckily work isn't like swimming, which means you don't need to wait half an hour before jumping back in," she said flippantly.

Obliging her interpretation of a request to return to work, we all filed out of the cafeteria without so much as a smart-aleck remark. Feeling as though our spirit had been broken at the mere sight of Mr. Desmond's sadistic orientation, we couldn't imagine how the younger boys felt at the hands of the all-powerful sociopath. As it was futile to dwell on something we absolutely had no power over changing, we took our axes, marched back up the ridge, and took out our resentment on the innocent forest, one tree at a time. It was actually quite therapeutic to chop down a tree while feeling resentful of authority since we were given the liberty to take down a towering giant. I don't know about the rest of my fellow campers, but I imagined the tree as Mr. Desmond as I hacked away at his ankles until he helplessly fell to the ground.

6

Counselor Arnold instructed us to drop our axes as he had an announcement regarding the work detail. Having to speak in an unnaturally loud tone to speak over the audible panting from the group of fatigued lumberjacks trying to catch their breath, she informed us with a somber tone that,

"A new development has been undertaken by the Flint Ridge administrative board, which means all new arrivals are to be diverted to a separate location."

Unaware of the implications of this update, the disheartened silence of my fellow campers was broken as Counselor Arnold continued to speak.

"So, rather than helping us clear our goal of twenty acres by summer's end, the extra manpower will have to be shared over the next thirteen weeks," she explained. "This means that we will have to extend our working hours by two: one in the morning and one in the evening."

Upon hearing the extension of already long and tiring workdays, Counselor Arnold tried to calm down the uproar of unenthusiastic campers. Unwilling to give an extra two hours of involuntary servitude per day, Counselor Arnold sympathized with our complaints. Understanding that forcing teenage boys to work thirteen hours a day of hard labor was excessive and would inevitably result in physical burnout, not to mention rightful defiance, she expressed her disdain for the decision.

"I get it and I'm not happy about it either," she said in genuine agreement. "Just understand that this decision is above my pay grade."

Providing little to no comfort knowing that Counselor Arnold was not spearheading the extension, we continued to voice our outrage.

"This is complete bull shit!" Finn remarked.

"This will fuckin' kill me!" Slim Jim added.

Counselor Arnold ignored the profanity and assuaged their hyperbolic concerns by saying, "Before you get all bent out of shape, rest assured that you're not in this alone. I promise I'll help clear trees every day in hopes of returning the schedule to a more realistic time frame."

Before we could question her commitment, Counselor Arnold immediately put her muscles where her mouth was and picked up her own axe. She ventured into the forest where she began channeling her own anger into leveling monstrous Sequoias. Showing us a sign of good faith, we recognized her dedication to us as a team and felt good to know that not all adults working in social services were our enemies.

After about an hour of hearing incessant chopping, chips of

wood flying against other tree trunks, and thuds of successfully chopped trees, Counselor Arnold tried to pick up the momentum and simultaneously lift our spirits. Progressing at a much quicker pace than the rest of us mere mortals, she hollered back at us with an unusual comment.

"You know what's missing here? Music!" She said playfully. Confused by the random remark, and not sure where she was going with the uncharacteristically bizarre observation, we remained quiet.

"C'mon guys, everyone knows music makes work more enjoyable!" She said trying to convince us of her motivational technique. "Someone start us off!"

Hesitant to her invitation to begin singing, we refrained from indulging the odd request. Continuing to chop away, she warned us,

"Fine, be like that. You'll be sorry when I pick the song," she said with a chuckle.

Still, we felt as though it was a trap, and any song we suggested would be met with an insult or form of mockery for the type of music we enjoyed. Unwilling to wait for us to muster the courage to engage in forest karaoke, she took the lead and began exclaiming the words to Devo's 1981 hit, "Working in a Coal Mine".

Beginning to sing a classic song we had never heard of due to our age and interest in popular music from this century, we were stunned as we heard Counselor Arnold rhythmically chanting the lyrics to the '80s pop hit.

"…Oops, about to slip down!" She sang with an animated tone.

Looking at one another to see if anyone would allow

themselves to be uninhibited enough to sing along with the catchy chorus, most of us froze before voluntarily being the first to try our hand at matching Counselor Arnold's surprisingly melodic vocals.

Ignoring our desire to be brooding adolescents rather than inspired singers, she bellowed the lyrics, echoing each verse off the ridge, bouncing off the trees that surrounded us, like a musical pinball game.

By the time she had ended the first rendition of the entire song, she began to re-start with the first verse as if the needle on the vinyl of her internal record player had been skipping, unable to start the next song on the LP. To clarify my basic knowledge of vinyl records, the musical medium had disappeared for most of my life but reappeared just before my stint at Flint Ridge. It turned out to only be a fad, but was nonetheless an interesting way of listening to our favorite songs compared to the impressive technology we use today. As Devo's classic hit was starting over, the song Counselor Arnold had been singing as a solo number had turned into a duet as Slim Jim sang along at the top of his water balloon-sized lungs.

"Workin' in a coal mine, goin' down down down," he sang with gusto.

Hearing the pop song for the first time, Jim impressively sang along, repeating the lyrics after Counselor Arnold finished each verse. As Jim and Counselor Arnold bellowed the song, they continued to hack away at their trees in a productive rhythm. Noticing how enjoyable it looked to turn a mind-numbingly repetitive task into an exciting musical experience, I joined in the musical round after they both had passed the second "Oops, about to slip down" verse. As I tried not to fumble the words of the song, I used my limited musical ability to keep up with Jim, who appeared to have a natural talent for singing. Before we knew it, the entire lot of campers started to join in, starting as barely audible humming, escalating into an incomprehensible mumbling, then finally blasting into passionately echoing chanting. I don't how many times we sang the same song on a loop, but we repeated the chorus out of order when we felt like it, then jumped between verses. It really didn't matter to us or Counselor Arnold, we just sang until our hearts were content, forgetting for a brief moment that we were prisoners at Flint Ridge.

 Realizing that we had sung the song to death at the sight of Counselor Arnold's face as she visibly dreaded singing another verse of the song she had instigated, we all burst out in laughter as Jim continued to belt out the words. Catching Jim off guard as we ceased singing in unison, he looked around for a moment to see what had caused our inexplicable silence, then took it upon himself to transition into his personal favorite.

 Without skipping a beat, he seamlessly began singing "Swing Low, Sweet Chariot," a traditional song first made popular nearly a century before our time. As the small boy embodied the hauntingly beautiful, yet oppressed voice of what sounded like a middle-aged chain gang worker from the nineteen-forties, we stopped our chopping to keep our jaws from hitting the forest floor. Stunned by his powerhouse voice, we continued to watch him in awe, unable to understand how such a tiny person could produce such an enormous voice. As he finally opened his eyes following the completion of the song, truly feeling every note he sang, he realized he had an active audience. Waiting a moment to let Jim's impressive musical talent sink in, we then exploded in applause, cheering, and hollering. The louder we cheered and whistled at Jim, the more bashful he became, turning his head toward his tree to hide his blushing cheeks.

Equally impressed by Jim's voice, Counselor Arnold exclaimed that he would lead us as his backup vocals the next day and he got to choose which song we all sang. Excited by the news, Jim put us all in a fit of laughter as he suggested without so much as a self-conscious thought,

"You should all brush up on The Bee Gees because tomorrow we're singing 'Stayin' Alive.'"
Even Counselor Arnold burst out into laughter as we tried to wrap our heads around Slim Jim's eclectic musical taste.

As if we were surrounded by friends and family, we continued to laugh with a blissful distraction from the reality of where we were. That is, until Mr. Desmond appeared to cruelly bring us back to our abysmal reality. With Paul trailing behind him like a malevolent shadow, Mr. Desmond sternly addressed Counselor Arnold. In a leading manner, he asked,

"Why does it sound as if y'all are enjoying an evening at a karaoke bar rather than getting some work done?" Falsely implying that he could hear us all the way from the main hall.

Counselor Arnold explained cautiously, "We were working. Just making the day a bit more bearable, Mr. Desmond."

Interrupting in an accusatory manner, Mr. Desmond said, "Perhaps your time would be best spent enforcing rather than trying to win a popularity contest." Then continued to patronize Counselor Arnold, "It's apparent I should have trusted my instincts before hiring you. Besides the overt red flags."

"What exactly do you mean by that?" Counselor Arnold said defensively.

"Exactly as you're exemplifying at this very moment," he said aggressively. "Obviously you cannot be in a position of power with unnatural passive female hormones coursing through your body."

Trying to mask the hurt Counselor Arnold felt in response to the insulting remarks, she once again tried to defend herself, which was met with ignorant condescension from Paul, who had been waiting his turn to berate her.

Paul viciously attacked Counselor Arnold's competency by stating,

"If a real woman can't lead with an iron fist, it makes sense that a fake woman would be even less capable."
As an expression of self-doubt and shame washed over Counselor Arnold's once brave face, she responded as I expected she had been forced to most of her life: with a non-confrontation passivity. Knowing that it would be futile to defend herself in the face of such ignorance, she said,

"I'm sorry you both feel that way," apologizing softly. "We'll get back to work…quietly.

Happy to oblige her order, we all got back to chopping and tried to ignore the bullying presence that lurked over our shoulders. Counselor Arnold turned her back toward a tree, in part to avoid confrontation, but also to hide the tears in her eyes that accumulated as a result of justified anger. Unfortunately, her attempt at subtly prompting Mr. Desmond and his lackey to go about their business was met with more intolerance.

Snickering at each other like petty school children taught to harass those appearing different than themselves, Paul encouraged Mr. Desmond's distasteful comments with spine-chilling cackling. As they made snide comments in a tone loud enough for Counselor Arnold to hear over her chopping, they escalated the severity of their comments until Paul shouted in a most unforgivable fashion, "I bet you won't be able to swing an axe that hard when you get your fake tits and pussy installed."

Shocked by the inappropriately crude insult, Counselor Arnold had reached her breaking point as her tears dried up, channeling her sadness into pure hatred. She swung the axe over her shoulder, then started walking towards Mr. Desmond and Paul, who continued to ridicule her with dehumanizing remarks as she confidently walked over to them. As she passed by, I followed behind her to show my support even though she was so focused that she didn't recognize I had been at her side until we reached the cackling duo.

First intending to use her words to diffuse the situation, while asserting her demand for respect, Counselor Arnold simply stated,

"I don't appreciate your comments and would prefer if you kept her work environment a respectful and dignified one."

Unwilling to accept her desire to be treated in a fair manner any person deserved, Paul mercilessly refused to acknowledge her rights by expressing another unjust slur.

"Relax, freak," he said coldly.

Upon hearing yet another disgraceful comment, Counselor Arnold lost her patience and approached Paul within an inch of his face,

"I think I deserve an apology," she said while gritting her teeth.

As her face neared his, Paul's intolerance grew fiercely, provoking him to push Counselor Arnold away, once again calling her a freak. I stood behind Counselor Arnold as I watched a blatant act of social injustice take place before my eyes. I could not bear to see the only respectable staff member at Flint Ridge being talked to with such disrespect. Finally noticing my presence behind her, Counselor Arnold intervened as she saw my fist flying through the air, directed squarely at Paul's face.

Grabbing my fist before it could make contact with Paul's smug grimace, Counselor Arnold pushed against the force of my arm and lowered it to my side. As Mr. Desmond gestured for Paul to grab hold of me and punish me for my intent to cause harm to a guard, Counselor Arnold forcefully walked me past them with my arm securely behind my back.

"Not to worry, Mr. Desmond. Hunter will spend the remainder of the day in The Pit as punishment," she said with a cooperative demeanor.

Rushing me up the ridge before Paul or Mr. Desmond could reach me and implement a more severe and injurious punishment, Counselor Arnold whispered to me as she gently placed her hand on my shoulder,

"You need to work on your impulse control."

Although Counselor Arnold made it clear that my actions were myopic and would not have remedied the ignorance displayed by Paul, her tone expressed more gratitude than she would ever admit. Once we made it back to the bunkers, I veered to the right in anticipation of revisiting the solitude of being locked away in The Pit. To my confusion, Counselor Arnold instead directed me to turn left and brought me into a secluded part of the overgrown woods, one I hadn't cared to visit since arriving at Flint Ridge, assuming it was a breeding ground for mosquitos and poison ivy. Proving my assumptions to be partially correct, I was instantly swarmed with mosquitos, buzzing around my ears before landing on my bare neck to drain me of my youthful blood. Irritated by the itchy welts left behind by the blood-thirsty flying pests, we pushed aside hanging branches and ventured past the many natural obstructions into a small clearing.

As I tried to swat away the relentless mosquitos with one hand while I brushed away the ineffective cobwebs from my face with the other, I was led to a small space located in the middle of the forest. Cleared of trees and bushes, this six feet by six feet clearing had a single punching bag hanging from a sturdy horizontal branch above. Walking up to the duct-taped red bag, hypnotically swaying from the breeze rocking the rusted chains that supported the hefty piece of athletic equipment, Counselor Arnold shared the purpose of our detour.

"This punching bag has allowed me to direct his anger when

humiliated by ignorant people like Mr. Desmond and Paul," she explained. She continued by saying, "While it's hard to avoid hateful people, retaliating with violence is just giving them what they want."

Explaining a fundamental rule for dealing with aggression, one I hadn't ever been taught, she urged me to consider an alternate course of action next time I am provoked.

"Don't raise your fist to people who enjoy raising their own fist back," she suggested. "To aggressive people, passivity is a foreign language. So, when you keep your cool and walk away from confrontation, they will be confused by your unwillingness to engage in violence. This is a talent held only by the most enlightened people, and believe me, you'll get more satisfaction by staying calm than by getting bloody knuckles."

Understanding that it wasn't an easy task to forge new paths in my already mapped neuropathways, Counselor Arnold tried to show me the satisfaction that results from knowing when to walk away. She pointed at the large punching bag and said that the huge vinyl sack filled with dense sand had saved her job countless times by allowing her to release her frustration without injuring anyone, including herself.

Without saying another word, she positioned herself like a professional boxer and began pummeling the punching bag with well-executed blows up and down the shaking bag. As the momentum from the force of Counselor Arnold's fury-fueled fists rocked the branch above, she took one last cathartic swing, then held onto the bag to keep it from swaying into the wee hours of the night. She then shared a part of her past she hadn't cared to verbalize in quite some time.

"You know, I used to box professionally as a man, but then was prevented from competing once I began hormone therapy," she shared candidly.

Knowing very well that she wouldn't be received with open arms in the women's boxing league due to her biological sex, Counselor Arnold made the hard decision to walk away from boxing and utilize her time once spent in the ring to begin her social work degree, working towards battling the issues inferred by troubled youth.

She stepped away from the punching bag, heaving her chest with every deep breath she took. Then, she invited me to take a turn hitting the bag that exceeded both my weight and height. I tried to mimic her professional-looking stance, then threw a punch as I pictured Paul's infuriating face. Throwing a right hook, my fist barely made contact with the still bag, but still managed to twist my wrist in an unnatural motion. Retracting my arm as a pain shot up to my elbow, Counselor Arnold asked me to wait while she bent over to retrieve an old pair of brown leather boxing gloves that had been sitting on a nearby tree stump. Like my memories of the summer spent at Flint Ridge, those gloves have also stayed with me for the past fifty years. Despite the tree stump on which they were stored every day that summer, I now keep them hanging on a wall-mounted hook in my den at home, surrounded by pictures of me standing next to welterweight champions in various boxing rings around the country. Wearing the gloves bestowed onto me by Counselor Arnold protected my hands as I fought hundreds of worthy opponents during every one of my professional matches.

Although I would eventually learn how to properly lace boxing gloves early on in my boxing career, Counselor Arnold sensed I didn't have the slightest inclination as to what I was doing. Holding one glove between her thighs while she secured the first glove on my right hand, she then put my left hand in the second glove before giving me my first lesson on how to throw a punch that wouldn't break my wrist. Enthusiastic to learn, I listened intently while Counselor Arnold gave me tips on how to stand and extend my arms. I jabbed at that punching bag while my new coach gave me valuable tips that I would use every time I stepped into a boxing ring. Without them, I wouldn't have had the confidence or skills to win one fight, let alone bring home a championship belt in 2035.

She took the bag with both hands, then shoved it to create a swinging motion. As I instinctually leaned forward to hit it as it got farther away, Counselor Arnold corrected me by saying that I should resist the urge to hit the bag right away and anticipate a more opportune shot. As it started to swing back in my direction, she told me to hit it from the side. Obeying her coaching technique, I followed through and connected with the bag, sending it flying to the side. Hitting the bag as well as I did, I watched with pride as the large bag rapidly spun in circles, binding the chains together, then spinning it in the opposite direction while the supporting branch shook like a jackhammer. She smiled as if to acknowledge my quick progress, and then reiterated her mantra from the previous day, stating "Foresight yields hope." Beginning to understand the meaning behind her philosophy, I took the saying to heart and suspected that Counselor Arnold was more insightful than I initially gave her credit.

We continued to dance around the bag for hours, so focused that we even missed the buttered noodles that waited for us in the dining hall. Once the night sky encompassed the forest and we had difficulty seeing the swinging punching bag, we decided to give it a break for the night and continue the lesson after work the next day. Not only did we pick up where we left off that day, but we also intended on meeting every evening for at least an hour of intensive boxing lessons, exercising different muscle groups and skillsets that ultimately allowed me to be taken seriously when I returned to my neighborhood as an amateur boxer.

Having been given the skills to fight as a respected athlete rather than a street kid with a violent temper, I had unknowingly received the first form of constructive discipline that would help me stay on the path toward a good life. Admittedly, I did veer off that path from time to time in my adult life, but I always managed to get myself back on track (sometimes with more difficulty than I would have liked). In addition to receiving my first lesson to control my rampant negative emotions, thereby channeling them through the art of boxing, there was a positive side effect. By the time we finished hitting the punching bag, I was completely exhausted and looking forward to getting some much-needed shut-eye for the first time since Lucky had died.

On top of the rewarding aches from an intense workout, what I liked most about boxing was that the punching bag didn't hit back, leaving me feeling a satisfactory kind of pain rather than one associated with defeat. So, I carried my aching body up the dilapidated steps of Bunker Eight and once again crept to my bed without waking the others. Relieved to finally crawl into bed, I kicked around under my sheets in case I had been the victim of another disgusting practical joke, then happily curled up under the sheets in exhaustion.

A couple of hours into my blissful slumber, I was awoken by an itchy sensation on my pinky finger. In a sleep-deprived state, I tried to keep my eyes closed to convince myself that I was going straight back to sleep. Reaching under my pillow with weak arms from the day's work, I vigorously scratched the knuckle of my pinky finger until the irritation subsided. For a few seconds, the itchiness seemed to be relieved, but then returned as a burning sensation coursing down my finger to my wrist. Continuing to worsen the skin irritation from more scratching with my soil-encrusted nails, it felt as though my entire hand had been immersed in pink fiberglass insulation. Wrongfully accusing the rampant mosquito population of the rising welts on my hand, I cursed the buzzing blood suckers and threw the comforter over my head and hands to prevent any more flying insects from enjoying a midnight snack quite literally on me.

Once I had cocooned myself under the wool blankets, creating what I thought to be an impenetrable shield against tiny winged invaders, I was able to fall back asleep with little distraction from my throbbing hand. Just as soon as my mind ignored the irritation, allowing me to return to an unhindered state of unconsciousness, I was rudely awakened again by the same itchiness, but this time it was on the right side of my torso. Feeling the two separate irritated areas, I first ran my fingers down my blisteringly hot skin and felt three bumps in a staggered line. Then, I took my left arm and reached under my body to feel my side, which also had three distinct bumps along the flesh that touched the coarse fitted sheet underneath. Growing insane from frustration, I wrapped myself tightly in the blankets like a hand-rolled cigar and drifted off for the third time that night. Falling prey to the suspected ingenuity of hungry mosquitos, my resting head was once again raised in alarm as now my toes were experiencing the same intense irritation as my finger and side. Reaching down to swat away any lingering mosquitos, I grabbed hold of a wingless insect crawling along the sole of my foot. Making a fist with the unidentified insect in the middle of my clenched hand, I slowly opened it to see what had been causing my sleepless night. When I opened my hand, flattening my palm as an unobstructed display for the minuscule night crawler, it was a brown, oval-shaped bug with a tiny head, one I had the displeasure of rooming with at Eleanor and Perry's house.

    Being no stranger to being victimized by stealth, resilient bed bugs at my infested home, my skin crawled in response to seeing yet another one of the unholy pests. I realized with a heavy heart what had been biting me with carefully planned mealtimes as my breathing regulated. I unknowingly invited the insect squatters to feed on my seventeen-year-old aged blood, like a highly-sought after vintage red wine. Sitting up in my bed with a heavy head, I could see through the dim light in the cabin that the rest of the campers were engaged in a futile battle of persistent scratching followed by tossing and turning. There was no doubt that there was an infestation in the cabin and just like my neglectful aunt and uncle, I was assured there would be no costly fumigation or extermination process whatsoever taking place in the near future. The combination of equally stale clothes and sheets rank with teenage body odor, not to mention the absence of a washer or drier located anywhere on the campgrounds, made it apparent that cleanliness was not a priority of the Flint Ridge administration. As I was forced to do at Eleanor's house, I had to keep my aversion to nightly insect awakenings as a riled-up inner monologue, never to complain about the infestation to an adult who would accuse me of being paranoid and sensitive; neither of which I considered myself to be.

    As soon as my drooping eyelids closed following the final bed bug invasion, I was once again awake. My mind woke preemptively before the morning fire cracker was lit. Envious of the others, who could somehow enjoy a full night's sleep, I resisted the temptation to vigorously rock the bunkbeds on my way out while screaming to imply there was an earthquake. Instead, I quietly rose from the bed and walked out without disturbing the others to avoid warranting another retaliatory prank. Forgetting how cold the country mornings were, the brisk air that seeped through the wire mesh made me reconsider leaving my warm blanketed bed. Having come too far, I braved the cold and carefully opened the door, leading me to enjoy the serene views in absolute solitude and silence.

    Admiring the eerily thick fog that hung in the chilled air, I sat on the cracked porch steps feeling as though I was embraced by a cloud. Unable to see more than a few feet in any direction, I was comforted by the anonymity that the fog brought. Veiled by the mist that rolled in over the mountains, pooling down in the valley, I dreaded the rising morning sun coming up over the eastern horizon as its rays burned the fog away. Through the dense fog, I could only hear a rustling coming from the nearby bushes to the side of Bunker Eight. Unknowledgeable of the local wildlife in the area, I naively walked over, following the distressing sound in hopes of discovering a never-before-seen animal. Unaware of the presence of grizzly bears, mountain lions, and coyotes roaming the foothills of Flint Ridge and Valley, I walked up to the trembling bush with ignorance-based confidence as if I was on an African safari. Stumbling on the way due to my impaired vision amidst the heavy fog, tripping on exposed roots, and losing my footing in rabbit holes, I got close enough to the shrubbery to realize it was not a predator capable of tearing me limb from limb, but a defenseless dog.

    The stray dog looked like a cross breed between a basset hound and a husky; it had a full coat of grey fur hanging down past its short stubby legs. Marked with black patches of fur down its long back from its pointed tail to its floppy raggedy ears, this dog was the most handsome canine I had ever witnessed. Through the fog, the haze made me feel like I was dreaming. I had always wanted a dog as a faithful companion and this one seemed to be conjured out of my own favorite characteristics of various dogs I had admired growing up. Never fully comfortable with the idea of bringing a vulnerable pet into Eleanor and Perry's house as a child, I couldn't imagine what they would have done to a puppy if they had no aversion to hurting a child with such passionate indifference. Consequently, I never even asked for a dog, sparing the defenseless creature a lifetime of cowering in fear as its owner faced daily.

Simultaneously ecstatic and heartbroken to have stumbled upon my dream dog, I kneeled down to greet the aging dog. As I got closer, I could tell that the rustling I had heard was a result of his back paw being tangled in the brush. Held captive by the natural equivalent of barbed wire, the scared dog was trying with little success to pry his paw free from the irritating thorns. Upon first sight of this miraculous dog, I knew I would do anything to keep him happy and out of harm's way, so I reached down to loosen the prickly noose secured tightly around his sore paw. As I touched his tender paw, the dog lifted it from the ground to relieve some pressure from the wound, then nervously tried to nip at my hand to prevent me from exacerbating the injury. I reassured the frightened dog by brushing the wispy grey hair on his adorably long ears with one hand, while I delicately removed his paw with the other. With a minimal struggle, the dog lifted his paw from the thistles but didn't go far.

Wagging his tail in gratitude, the elderly dog circled around to thank me for freeing him by nuzzling his white-haired snout between my legs. Trying to jump up on me to lick my face as a reward for helping him out, he limped on his back paw from the recently inflicted pain of the thorny bush. Assuming there were a couple of lacerations around the dog's right ankle from the slight traces of blood on his wild grey fur, I bent down to allow him to lick my face without exerting as much effort. In a state of unprecedented bliss, I ran my fingers through the dog's thick coat as he licked every inch of my face clean of the dirt and dried sweat from the previous night's boxing lesson. Unnecessarily repaying his debt for my assistance earlier, the nameless dog panted with his tongue hanging to the side of his jowls, adding to the mist as his hot breath reacted to the cold air.

Excited by my newfound companion, I walked over a couple of feet to the bush in which he had been stuck and broke off the largest branch I could find, then raised it over my head. It was not my intention to tease the dog, but before I could throw it and engage in a long-awaited game of fetch with the affable dog, I remembered he had a sore paw and did not want to aggravate the injury with gratuitous running. Overwhelmed by the anticipation of being gifted a glorious branch, the dog sat on the ground with perfect posture, wagging his tail so vigorously that the grass flew in the air as if a whipper snipper had been taken to it. He then let out the most heartwarming howl I could have imagined.

To avoid having the dog run on his hurt paw, I simply dropped the branch in his mouth, prompting him to anxiously snap at it mid-air. As he played with his treasured toy, thrashing it about in his mouth, then pawing at it on the ground as if it would come alive and play with him, I grabbed hold of one end and played tug of war with my new friend. Losing all track of time as I frolicked in one place with the one thing in the world that mattered to me, I was disheartened as we were both startled by the unexpected bang of the morning firecracker alarm being lit from within Bunker Eight. Feeling threatened by the startling sound, the dog whimpered and ran into the forest to protect himself from what he probably assumed was a gunshot. The gun-shy canine left me behind holding his new favorite chew toy, whole-heartedly disappointed by our short visit with each other. I only hoped that he would return to play and allow me to give him the kind of unconditional love I hadn't ever had the opportunity or pleasure of giving.

    I returned to Bunker Eight to watch the group of fatigued campers file out of the cabin sporting disheveled hair with age-inappropriate bags under their puffy eyes. All of whom sported aged, stress-induced visages indicative of middle-aged, worn-down men. They retrieved their axes from the exterior wall of the log cabin and lethargically walked up the ridge for an active day filled with cutting down enormous trees. As my fellow campers started to wake up after about an hour of strenuous physical labor, Slim Jim led us like an unholy choir as he began to sing the Bee Gees' disco hit, "Stayin' Alive," staying true to his promise following his breakout performances the previous day. Unable to focus on the incomprehensibly high-pitched lyrics of the day, I mouthed a string of vowels on a loop to disguise my disinterest in singing. Instead, my attention belonged to my morning companion, hoping his paw was healing nicely in hopes that he would remember me as trustworthy enough to return for some more tug of war or even a game of fetch if he felt up to it.

    In case I were lucky enough to see that pure-hearted mutt again, I felt that it was only right to give him a name. I figured that if some of the world's most despicable individuals were loved enough to be given a name, such as Paul or whichever given name the Desmond family bestowed onto their demon spawn, an animal of such honorable character deserved an identity. As I racked my brain trying to pick the perfect name to properly exemplify the innocence that my new friend exuded, I ruled out any generic pet name like Pal, Spot, or Buddy. I then disregarded names that made dogs sound uncharacteristically mean or ruthless, like Rex, Chomper, or Cujo. Meticulously going through a mental list of male names for a dog, like I was naming a newborn, I came to the conclusion that this dog meant more to me than any human ever did, which is why he deserved a human's name. Since I was never star-struck by celebrities or valued the persona of a public figure enough to pay homage in that particular way, I decided to name him Joe after my dearly departed friend, Joe "Lucky" Conners. After associating the name Joe with the angelic face I had the pleasure of playing with earlier that morning, it soon became the obvious choice; the dog just seemed like a Joe and coincidentally had stubby legs as Lucky did. Entertaining the idea of simply calling the dog Lucky, which is more of a typical name for a dog, I dismissed it as I superstitiously did not want to pass on the ironic fate.

By the time I had confidently named Joe, I had mindlessly cut down two trees and realized that the rest of the gang had sung their way through the morning set list, ending the morning with another disco classic, Gloria Gaynor's "I Will Survive." Impressed that hours had passed without giving it so much as a thought, it was already ten thirty, meaning it was meal time.

Strangely enough, I had worked up so much of an appetite during my morning of distracted tree chopping that I was actually looking forward to the suspected styrofoam textured disc of stale bread being passed off as pizza. My appetite faded as soon as I walked into the dining hall and smelled the familiar, unappetizing aromas of burnt syrup and boiling pork overpowering the scentless pizza. I knew I couldn't wait for buttered noodles, as I feared I would collapse due to malnutrition, I took a few bites of the grotesque medley even though it tasted even worse than I cared to imagine. Unable to power through the taste for sheer satiation, I gave up on the distasteful dish and decided to pick out small pieces of what might have been slivers of pepperoni in hopes that Joe would have less of a picky appetite than myself. I discretely stuffed the rock-hard encased meat in the pockets of my sweatpants without Lucille noticing, then quickly dumped out the disappointing pizza in the trash can in the corner of the dining hall while she hacked up her remaining lung onto the serving container behind the counter.

Once we were ready to head back to the forest, picking up both our axes and where Slim Jim had left off in his nineteen-seventies playlist, a shuffle of boys from Bunker Seven sluggishly walked into the dining hall for their meal. Most of the pre-teen campers were on the brink of tears, looking as though they were run ragged worse than us, even with our extended days. Avoiding eye contact with us out of fear of the suspected wrath of interacting with senior campers, they kept their eyes focused on the serving counter. Unwilling to utter a word to each other in our presence, they silently accepted their meal and nervously chose their seats at either of the long log tables. As we observed them eating their modern-day gruel without hesitation, it appeared as though the fear in their eyes were not only a result of our intimidating presence.

Simultaneously possessing the same morbid suspicion, we

scanned the room for the abused child we had witnessed the previous day. Distraught by his absence, we feared the worst but humored ourselves by assuming he was either sent home out of sympathy or relieved of work detail due to the medical opinion of Nurse Bea. Although we found the optimistic scenarios difficult to believe, it was the only way we could escape the realistic fear that our lives were in jeopardy.

As we returned to the slowly diminishing forest to continue our day's work, my mind was elsewhere. Unable to think about the well-being of the unknown Bunker Seven resident who mysteriously went missing following a powerful blow from Mr. Desmond's knee. I was instead preoccupied with the well-being of Joe, my newly adopted pet. Out in the wilderness all alone without shelter to call home, I worried about Joe and his ability to survive the harsh elements of the countryside. Falling prey to life-threatening predators, including ill-willed humans, Joe was at the mercy of his environment and I couldn't bear to think of him having to fend off veritable monsters while in such a weakened state.

Proving to be an effective way to pass time, my rumination brought me through the afternoon until we were dismissed from the forest. As we waited for Lucille to make her way over to the serving counter, I had little hope for the chef's daily special of buttered noodles, so I didn't bother to wait in line and chose instead to sit outside while the rest of the group stomached the suspected continued insult to Italian cuisine. Not to sound like a food snob, seeing as how my favorite meal is still boxed macaroni and cheese, but even my underdeveloped palate could differentiate between cheap food and the garbage they served at Flint Ridge. Opting out of my plate of what I assumed was shredded newspaper drenched in melted lard labeled as buttered noodles, I decided to go sit outside and escape the awful smell that billowed from the kitchen.

Hoping to get an early reunion with Joe, I stood on the splintering steps of the dining hall and surveyed the area to see if I could get a glimpse of another trembling bush or an excitingly wagging tail far off in the distance. To no avail, Joe was nowhere to be found, and I was left wondering where he could be and worried about his safety. Fixated on Joe, I had forgotten about my own unfavorable circumstances and how I was also subject to the harsh environment of Flint Ridge. Just as I would later come to experience as a parent, when my kids were in trouble, my own issues paled in comparison. Even though Joe and I seemed to be stranded in the same boat, navigating the treacherous waters inhabited by inhumane creatures, I felt more capable of taking care of myself. As I waited in anticipation like a parent whose child missed curfew, time had quickly passed and I had to abandon my lookout to return to the forest for the remainder of the work day.

As the rest of the day passed by as quickly as ever, going through the motions of clearing trees and learning how to box with Counselor Arnold, I could not shake the feeling that Joe had gotten into some sort of trouble. Regretting how I just let him leave in fear rather than try to call him back and keep him safe, I was stricken with guilt as I took on the responsibility of ensuring that Joe stayed alive and well.

All through the night, I laid awake with insomnia, imagining awful ways in which Joe could have gotten hurt by getting caught on another thorn bush, falling down the ridge from a rockslide, or running into a ferocious bear. All of those scenarios were equally troublesome and they made it impossible for me to get any sleep while the other boys snored peacefully around me. Catching a glimpse of the dawn's early light shining through the window at the front of the cabin, casting a shadow of the screen door on the center of the room, I hopped out of bed to see if Joe had returned.

    Anxious to see if Joe had remembered where we had met, I paced back and forth all over the campground in hopes of leaving my scent around the area so he could find me. When I had finally given up hope, coming to terms with yet another thing in life to be taken away, first Lucky, then freedom, and finally Joe, my eyes filled with tears of relief as I saw Joe running up to me from out of the forest. Howling in my direction as if he had been looking for me since the firecracker had scared him off, I bent down and greeted him as he jumped in my arms, placed his paws over my shoulder and eagerly licked my face. Amidst the excitement of reconnecting with my new best friend, I almost forgot to feed him the bits of pepperoni I had smuggled out of the dining hall but was reminded by Joe's impressive nose as he rooted around in my pocket. Happy to treat my companion to an early morning snack, I cupped the meat in my hand and let him eat from my palm while he drooled from my wrist to my fingertips.

    Wishing we had more time to play together, I anticipated Counselor Arnold's silence-shattering firecracker had led Joe to the clearing where I had my boxing lessons. Before leaving him alone, unwilling to make the same mistake of leaving him vulnerable in the woods, I hurried back to my bunk and retrieved the wool blanket that was neatly made atop my bed. Rushing back to Joe so he wouldn't feel abandoned, I brought him the blanket and bunched it up into a perfectly shaped dog bed for him to wait comfortably until I returned. I then hugged him around his mangy neck and promised him I would come back with breakfast at 10:30. Feeling an unfamiliar sense of what I deemed to be love when Joe let me hug him, I questioned my ability to love. For most of my life, I have felt that defensiveness and an openness to love were as compatible as oil and water. Always separating upon contact, the two entities were in essence fighting for dominance. In my case, love acted as the water, suppressed by the dominant defensiveness, making it impossible to rise through its dense surface.

7

Regardless of my perceived ability to truly love another being, I trusted that Joe would be safe while I was away. I left him with enough food and warmth to entice him into staying around at least until his paw healed. Reluctant to leave him behind, I had to get back to Counselor Arnold and the rest of the group before I endured an array of consequences for tardiness. Therefore, I rushed back to the dining hall to retrieve my axe, noticing that the rest of the axes had already been dislodged from the side of the cabin. Unable to estimate how long I had been preoccupied with Joe, I wasted little time in scaling the ridge, back to where I was expected. As I sprinted over the ridge, I could see that the rest of the campers were on their way to another location, leaving their axes behind. Following Counselor Arnold through the thick of the forest, I joined the group at the tail end of the line, hoping that my absence was not yet noticed.

Regrouping with Finn and Slim Jim at the back of the line, I was confused by the spontaneous change of scenery and curiously asked where we were headed. Finn explained that Mr. Desmond ordered Counselor Arnold to bring us down to where the kids from Bunker Seven were working to help out as they were making little progress. Forced to delay our own duties, subsequently ensuring that we would endure the consequences of not finishing our own work detail by the end of the summer, it was apparent that we were now encouraged to fail.

The farther we walked through the overgrown brush, the more I felt distanced from an educated guess as to where we were going and what we were expected to do once we got there especially since we didn't have any tools with us. After a forty-five-minute hike, exhausting the group before we even started the secret work for the evening, we arrived in a valley covered in knee-high weeds matched in height by mounds of dirt, immobilized boulders that had rolled to the absolute lowest point of the valley, and clusters of prickly pear cacti inconveniently placed around our feet. I hadn't even been aware that we were in a climate where cacti could thrive, but apparently the complexities of nature made it so.

When we arrived in the desolate wasteland, we could see the campers from Bunker Seven scattered around the vast area pulling weeds and working together to budge massive boulders up the steep incline. Shedding some light on the work detail for the younger campers, I believe I could speak for all of us when I expressed gratitude for being assigned to cutting down trees rather than tedious clean-up duty. We ventured down into the valley with Counselor Arnold as our lead, who greeted the other Counselor in charge of the children aged twelve to fourteen; we were told to call him Counselor Ray.

Counselor Ray was a man of few words and the few words he did mumble were never once addressing us directly, choosing instead to communicate with Counselor Arnold. Even then, he would only make active demands, such as "Arnold, send two campers over to the west perimeter asap." Not only did he not speak to us directly, portraying a sense of elitism that seemed more in line with the Flint Ridge mission statement than Counselor Arnold's accepting outlook on social class, he purposefully averted eye contact. If any one of us would cross into his field of vision, he would put on his black sunglasses, cross his arms, and look up at the sky as if he was asserting his dominance in the most peculiar way. It was actually quite humorous and we could tell that Counselor Arnold did not agree with his behavior by the way she shook her head in frustration every time he made an effort to treat the campers as inferior humans.

As we completed our orders relayed from Counselor Ray via Counselor Arnold, we assisted the understandably slow-moving Bunker Seven team in clearing the land for some unknown purpose.

Every bit of work we had completed since arriving at Flint Ridge had been riddled with obscurity, making certain that we could not envision the end product requiring countless hours of hard labor. Although clarity on the purpose of our daily activities would have been nice, it wouldn't have made the work any less grueling.

Down in the sunken valley, we were exposed to direct beams of sunlight absorbing into our exposed flesh, instantly burning our necks, faces, and arms. If the smoldering sun didn't provide enough discomfort, the abrasions from the razor-sharp weeds, piercings from the snapped branches, and bruises from uncoordinated run-ins with solid boulders left us in shambles by the end of the evening. Feeling the same amount of relief as though we had received a call from the governor sparing our lives from lethal injection, Counselor Arnold dismissed us back to our bunker for the night. We quickly ran up the hill in search of shade from the lingering, blistering evening sun before Counselor Ray instructed Counselor Arnold to call us back.

Huffing as we made our way back to the bunker to rest our scorched skin and scathed hands, we passive aggressively made our irritation known without warranting corrective measures by Counselor Arnold. In response to our audible huffs and unimpressed groans, she commented on the collective disdain for the change in work detail by acknowledging the unattractiveness of working in the valley.

"C'mon, Ray. Let's call it a day. The kids are beat," Arnold said trying to appeal to Counselor Ray's non-existent empathy.

"Well, they better get used to it," Ray explained. "Mr. Desmond has ordered all-hands-on-deck in the valley."

"This is the first I'm hearing of it," Arnold replied in frustration.

Counselors Arnold and Ray continued to speak to one another with irritation. Then, Counselor Arnod walked over to us to break the news, likely dreading our justified response.

"Listen, guys. As per the direct orders of Mr. Desmond, we will be spending half of each day down here assisting Bunker Seven in clearing the land."

Immediately met with opposition, we became increasingly resentful as she explained that each morning we would continue our regular work in the forest, but were expected to report to Counselor Ray after the morning lunch for back-breaking labor in the most unproductive conditions.

Except for a few muttered expletives that were ignored by Counselor Arnold as she considered the hostile responses to be understandable, we accepted the new challenging work schedule without a fight as incarcerated martyrs would. As we reached the cabin, seething from the incontestable work detail under the reign of Supreme Leader Ray and Dictator Desmond, the campers stomped into Bunker Eight angrily.

Before I could join my campmates in the cabin, Counselor Arnold pulled me away, saying that it was time for our boxing lesson. Although I tried to cancel the evening lesson and join the silent revolt of my peers, Counselor Arnold made the argument that even though I was rightfully tired and resentful, that was all the more reason to blow off some steam in a healthy forum. Realizing that she was not going to relent, I avoided wasting time debating the issue and unenthusiastically followed her to the clearing.

Making our way through the clearing to the punching bag, I realized that there was a strong possibility that Joe was still lying on the blanket waiting for me. Though I had not heard about a ban on pets at Flint Ridge, I suspected the privilege of having a dog was at least frowned upon, if not altogether prohibited. I was filled with dread thinking about putting Counselor Arnold in a predicament of having to report my secretive behavior to Mr. Desmond. The last thing I wanted to do was compromise the bond I had with her. Of course, I would also be subjecting myself to a multitude of inhumane punishments. So, I tried to make Joe's presence scarce by announcing our own by creating unhealthy sounds by clearing my unaffected throat and hacking up invisible phlegm. Just in case Joe had not gotten the hint, I purposefully stepped out of place on the driest branches in hopes that the cracking wood would send Joe running. As we approached the clearing, my heart started to race as Joe was nestled in the wool blanket, looking in our direction and wagging his tail in response to the exciting sounds indicating a long-awaited visit.

First puzzled by the presence of a dog curled up in a standard issue Flint Ridge wool blanket, Counselor Arnold stared at the drooling dog and quickly realized that I had some explaining to do.

"This is Joe," I explained meekly.

"Joe?" Counselor Arnold clarified.

"Yeah, he got hurt and I wanted to help get him better before finding his owner," I said dishonestly.

The last part was a creative lie that shined a good-hearted light on my actions as I had no intention of giving Joe back to his irresponsible and aloof owner. However, Counselor Arnold reacted more favorably than I had expected and walked over to Joe to rub his stomach. Enjoying the extra attention, Joe submissively rolled over on his back and aimed his four limp paws in the air. Instantly won over by Joe and his impressive ability to put anyone at ease, Counselor Arnold looked back at me with an annoyed look as he rolled his eyes. Acknowledging my disregard for a rule that apparently did exist, but understanding my urge to care for the angelic dog, she stood up and dragged the blanket to the side of the clearing. Acting as if we had not just reached power imbalance, she chose not to dwell on the blurred lines of being an ambiguous blend of coach, mentor, and counselor.

    Allowing Joe to stay and watch our boxing lesson, Counselor Arnold told me to put on my gloves and start hitting the bag slowly as a warm-up. Happy to oblige her instructions following a commendable decision to turn a blind eye towards my new pet, I started hitting the punching bag in appreciation. Focusing on my stance and well-executed strikes to distract Counselor Arnold from Joe, who began to playfully howl as I started to hit the bag, making it harder to ignore his endearing presence. Circling the swaying punching bag, I pivoted around as Counselor Arnold had taught me, a series of movements that Joe took as an invitation to join me. As I tried to punch the bag with Joe jumping up on me, while taking breaks to bite the bag to show his allegiance to me, Counselor Arnold waved her hands and told me to stop. Assuming she had second thoughts about nonverbally allowing me to keep Joe, I gestured to the dog to lie down at my feet. As the obedient dog settled down, Counselor Arnold started to massage her brow as if she was racking her brain with a suitable punishment for deceitfully hiding Joe, but then started to giggle inexplicably.

Walking over to us, Counselor Arnold ran his fingers through the dog's thick, curly fur and told me to take off the gloves. Worried that my boxing privileges were about to be revoked, I sulked as I untied the laces of the gloves with my teeth. Then, I was told to sit next to her as she continued to pet Joe, who couldn't be more relaxed by the mesmerizing massage he was being given. Finding a spot on the forest floor free from pine cones and rocks, I sat next to my mentor and dog.

"I'm proud of you, Hunter," Counselor Arnold said.

"Huh?" I replied in disbelief.

"You heard me. Joe needed someone to care for him as he healed and you stepped up," she said with a grin.

Upon hearing the word "healed," Joe obeyed the misunderstood homonym and abruptly sat upright, prompting an impressed cackle from Counselor Arnold.

She continued to say, "You showed heart, Hunter. Not only that, it tells me that you have character, and not just when it's convenient. I'm not oblivious to the fact that you've been dealt a raw deal and you probably weren't extended much empathy in your life."

"Not exactly, no," I said in agreement.

"And that's what makes you so special. You weren't taught to be a good person, Hunter, you just are," she said as she reached out to me.

Taken aback by Counselor Arnold's kind words, my eyes welled up; not from appreciation, but from guilt.

As I thought back to my recent troubled past involving Lucky and facilitating the end of his fourteen years of existence, I disagreed with Counselor Arnold's flattering observation. Not knowing whether to console me or ask for clarification regarding my rampant emotions, Counselor Arnold put her arm around my shoulder and expressed a kind of compassion that had been withheld from me by countless guardians, teachers, and friends. Intuitively guessing that my glassy eyes were a result of remorse rather than self-admiration, she bluntly addressed my tears.

"You're hurting and that's okay. But your past does not define you, it simply guides you," she said with confidence then added, "Fixating on the past is an act of futility that wastes energy that could be used to benefit yourself and others."

Urging me to live above my grief-stricken memories, she emphatically insisted that I regard my past as a mere lesson not to be forgotten, not a life sentence intended to limit my potential.

Sitting on the cold soil, Counselor Arnold embraced me, determined to squeeze out a tear from the bursting levees on my eyelids. As a single tear rolled down my chilled cheek, I swiftly wiped it away as a warning to the other pooling tears hesitant to overflow, which would confirm my vulnerability to act emotionally. Satisfied that I reached a heightened point of emotional maturity, Counselor Arnold changed the topic of conversation to evoke frustration, like she was arbitrarily pulling levers to test the functionality of various emotions.

Diverting my attention, she expressed how furious she was upon hearing of Mr. Desmond's dictatorial order to clear the landing at the bottom of the valley. She then mentioned how she found it cruel and torturous to subject children to that kind of grueling work, commenting on how she thought the work detail went beyond juvenile rehabilitation, teetering on the brink of cheap slave labor. Thinking aloud with conviction, she stated ambiguously, "Children should not be forced to make way for such morose developments."

Curious as to what developments Counselor Arnold was referring to with such contempt, I questioned her oversharing. Trying to backtrack, she stumbled on her words while she stood up trying to avert my attention back to boxing. Unwilling to let my curiosity roam free, I probed her for details, demanding with a grandiose sense of entitlement that it was my right to know. Snickering at my perceived level of entitlement, she gave me a look of astonishment as if I had allowed myself to believe such a delusion. Nevertheless, Counselor Arnold entertained my curiosity but swore me to secrecy as knowledge of Flint Ridge's plans was strictly restricted to staff. Explaining that if the other campers caught wind of the plans, her job would be as good as terminated and the developments would still be constructed regardless. Agreeing to keep the privileged information to myself, Counselor Arnold reluctantly disclosed the secret that had been eating her up inside.

"There would be a federal penitentiary built over the ridge where we had been clearing trees," she said with a sigh.

Unnerved by the idea of having adult felons in close proximity to suggestible youth, who already had a tendency to lean on the criminal side of the law, I could not comprehend how that development had been regarded as a viable concept.

"How could they do that?" I said outraged.

Counselor Arnold nodded her head in shared disbelief as she justified my concerns, but stated that Mr. Desmond's interests laid hand in hand with local politicians and businessmen who relished the idea of expanding a multi-age correctional facility on inexpensive land. Explaining that it was fiscally beneficial to utilize undesirable land (made so by the presence of the Flint Ridge Juvenile Detention Camp) to house criminals, Mr. Desmond happily accepted the proposal along with a substantial "finder's fee."

Having unburdened her mind about the socially questionable arrangement Mr. Desmond had made with local lawmakers and entrepreneurs alike, Counselor Arnold continued to divulge privileged information.

"That's the least of it," she said with a heavy heart. "The work assigned to the kids in Bunker Sever has an even more disgraceful purpose."

"How is that even possible?" I replied.

"The valley is the future site of a cemetery for deceased inmates who die in the custody of the future Flint Ridge maximum security federal penitentiary," Counselor Arnold explained.
Appalled by what I was hearing, she continued to explain that since most of the inmates were a burden to the government upon incarceration, most of their families (on the rare occasion that they had such a support system) would not identify, nor accept the bodies due to the incurred exorbitant costs associated with funerals.

Instead of paying for funeral costs out of their own pockets, the corporate owners of the prison discovered that developing an on-site graveyard would save massive amounts of funds by avoiding transportation and cremation expenses. The morbid kicker was that once the prison and cemetery areas were cleared by campers, future generations of remanded children would be assigned the task of digging shallow graves for the incarcerated dearly departed.

Regretting the divulgence of classified information, Counselor Arnold raised her tone of voice to a more reassuring pitch.

"Regardless of what happens, it's nothing for you to worry about. Before you know it, the summer will be over and you'll be back home," she said trying to console me.

Although she was correct in assuming that I wouldn't want to waste another thought on that godforsaken camp after that summer, I felt responsible for leaving behind a place unfit for children in need of ethical treatment and age-appropriate work duties. Not only that, what "home" was I supposed to be going back to? It certainly wasn't one that sparked anticipation.

As Counselor Arnold tried to persuade me into believing that the weight of any future Flint Ridge campers was heavier than any load my shoulders could bear, it was apparent that every one of h words fell onto my selectively deaf ears. Despite my lack of education regarding pertinent historic figures at the time, as I may have missed one or two high school history classes throughout my academic career, I spouted off the few names I remembered to cite precedence. I impressed both Counselor Arnold and myself by exclaiming passionately,

"Martin Luther King Jr. and John F. Kennedy didn't stand idly by while social integrity crumbled before their eyes".

Of course, that is how I would have said it speaking now, as an adult. I admit that the terms "idly" and "social integrity" were not part of my vocabulary at the time.

Understanding my outrage, Counselor Arnold finally leveled with me, unwilling to spare my feelings. She said with a saddened heart,

"It is honorable for me to care about other campers, but while you're still in the system as a juvenile delinquent, your words will not carry much weight on the scales of justice."

Drowned out by adults carrying a vested interest in real estate and the financial bottom line, the voice of a convicted youth might as well have been a whisper cast into a booming thunderstorm. Discouraged by the reality of my situation and the bottom-feeder economic status with which I had been classified, I turned to Counselor Arnold in hopes that she would carry the torch of my passionate crusade against social injustice.

"You need to do something," I pleaded.

Quick to agree that my convictions were justified and that nothing would make her happier than to stand up to a corrupt administration, Counselor Arnold quickly recanted her support. Looking at the situation pragmatically, she said,

"I know you mean well but I can't afford to put my job in jeopardy," she said humbly.

Sharing aspects of her personal budget without reservation, she stated that she depended on the unfairly small bi-weekly paychecks she received from Flint Ridge as her limited insurance plan made it hard to afford her hormone replacement therapy prescription. As much as she resented the establishment she worked for, the reality was that Flint Ridge paid her bills and allowed her to buy the estrogen and testosterone blocker medications that facilitated the ownership of her own identity.

Acting apathetically, I could not comprehend Counselor Arnold's perceived selfishness. Rather than help countless generations of abused children, she would stay dependent on a paycheck of dirty money to facilitate personal goals. As a teenager who had never had personal goals, a family, a budget, or real responsibilities of any kind, I was quick to judge Counselor Arnold's commitment to her own priorities. I was also unable to understand why Counselor Arnold felt compelled to work day and night for a disreputable organization in order to become her true self.

Looking back on that night, I feel ashamed to have treated her life goals as being inferior to the grand scheme of social justice for incarcerated youths. My inability to walk a few steps in another person's shoes to experience the discomfort of a life-long, worn-out sole made me ignorantly narrow-minded. Therefore, I acted selfishly and left in a huff, leaving Counselor Arnold with Joe to feel the unwarranted guilt of protecting her own interests. As I bolted through the forest to make my outrage known to all of the woodland inhabitants, I kicked and punched hanging branches out of my way, while Counselor Arnold rose above my inconsiderate actions.

"I'll bring a bag of dog food for Joe tomorrow morning," she said hoping to get me to come back.

I ignored her olive branch and left.

8

Fueled by hatred towards the establishment and Counselor Arnold's unwillingness to threaten the life she had planned for herself on the passionate whim of a seventeen-year-old boy, I marched straight to Bunker Eight, slamming the screen door behind me. Mistaking the abrupt sound of the wooden door colliding with the door frame as the morning firecracker alarm, Finn and Slim Jim jumped forward in their beds. Dreading the thought of another work day coming sooner than expected, they grumbled in their beds while the rest of the campers lied back down following the false alarm. Successfully provoking Finn and Jim to respond to my exaggerated hostility, I kicked the frame of my bunk bed before sitting down in a huff. Disturbing my upstairs bunkmate, my careless behavior was not appreciated, instigating a string of empty threats from above.

Realizing that the fuse leading to a fast-approaching emotional explosion had somehow been lit before I entered the cabin, Finn came over to de-escalate the confrontation before a brawl commenced. First, he told my bunkmate to go back to sleep, then he took me by the forearm to lead me out of the cabin before I could upset anyone else. Signaling to Slim Jim with a faint whistle to join us, he swung his legs out from under his covers, then flailed around as his short stature made it difficult for him to reach the floor the raised top bunk. Holding onto the edge of the bunkbed frame for dear life as if he was about to topple over the side of the Rockies, Jim finally let go and fell to the floor creating another loud nuisance that woke the exhausted campers from their slumber. Apologizing to the rest of the disgruntled cabin, Jim scurried out behind us before he was manhandled and thrown out for continuing to disrupt their much-needed sleep.

Standing on the porch in the middle of the night, only with the moonlight to outline our three silhouettes, we kept our voices down and our backs against the wall in case the Counselors decided to conduct an unannounced inspection. I turned to Finn to explain the cause of my outrage even though I was strictly ordered not to spread the news of the future prison and cemetery developments to anyone. But, it was obvious that he was uninterested in the cause of my anger anyway. Instead of actively listening to my concerns, Finn discretely pulled out a cell phone from the waistband of his sweatpants and placed his hand over the glaring light of the screen to block any giveaway that we were outside after lights out. He smiled a devilishly conniving grin as he speedily used his two thumbs to write a message on the contraband phone.

Once he finished the shortmessage, he held the screen to his chest to once again block the shining light indicating he had received a prompt response. Quickly reading the message before tucking it back between his stretched waistband and backside, he gave me and Jim little insight into his plan and simply ordered us to follow him. Reluctant to follow, Slim Jim stood on the structurally unsound porch, swinging his leg front to back off the step as if he was scared to jump off the high-dive at the community pool.

"Hurry up, Jim," Finn said. "You're not going to get in trouble. Plus, I need both of you for this to work."

Curious, yet left in the dark in regards to Finn's obviously defiant plans for the night, we blindly followed him in hopes of burning off some residual steam that the night's boxing lesson failed to do. Trailing behind us, Jim nervously stopped every few yards to point out nonexistent sounds and shadowed figures of Mr. Desmond and Paul in the distance. As Jim's paranoia began to irritate Finn, he finally turned around and told Jim to go back to the cabin before his next delusional word stomped on his last nerve. Having snuck past the main hall, we had already walked far down the gravel road, which made Jim change his attitude once he looked back towards the darkness, figuring that a walk back to the cabin alone was much more frightening than being caught by a superior.

As Finn walked ahead with his chest puffed out and his arms swinging side to side, as if he was on a life or death mission, I tried to have a conversation with Slim Jim to distract him from his overwhelming fear of being pegged as rebellious.

"So, what did you do to end up here?" I asked inquisitively.

"I listened to stupid Finn, same as you," Jim replied with impatience.

"No, I mean, what did you do to get sent to Flint Ridge?" I clarified.

Opposed to the mere thought of committing a crime, Jim was quick to defend his moral righteousness and explained that he had not been forced to spend the summer at Flint Ridge, clarifying that he was there strictly voluntarily.

"You chose to come here?" I asked with confusion. "Are you nuts?!"

Thinking that any person who would willingly spend their summer in a modern-day internment camp for kids was certifiably insane, I made my assumption of his insanity known. Rebutting my bold accusation, Jim explained confidently that he had chosen to go to Flint Ridge as a summer vacation to get away from the streets. Assuming that I knew what he was talking about as I identified myself as having frequented the city streets for most of my childhood, he humbly corrected me.

"No, you don't understand. I actually lived on the streets," he confessed.

"Oh," I replied at a loss for words.

Having fallen through the widening cracks within the shifting child services department, Slim Jim had been left without a home or guardian shortly before his fifteenth birthday. Exchanged between various overcrowded foster homes and apathetic government-run orphanages, his existence was overlooked between placement transfers, leaving him homeless. Relying solely on the benevolent nature of select citizens with spare change jingling in their shallow pockets, he was forced to provide for himself without an education, job, or community resources. He justified his contentment with being given the opportunity to spend a summer out in the country, enjoying clean air in a safe, comfortable cabin, while receiving two meals more than he was guaranteed each day. Turning the tables, Jim questioned my upbringing, alluding to the fact that I must have been delusional to think that I was entitled to a more accommodating camp.

Dumbfounded by the awareness that there was in fact a lower rung on the economic ladder than I had been accustomed to, I apologized for jumping to conclusions. My apology, however, was not accepted by Jim; not because he was bitter, but because he had a firm understanding of the social status and accepted his standing in the world. Before I could ask him why he was abandoned and where he suspected his biological parents had been (on the off-chance they were still alive), we approached the Flint Ridge barbed wire gate and caught a glimpse of what Finn had in store for the night.

Trying to keep our hanging jaws from plowing trenches in the gravel road, Jim and I lost all confidence and coordination as we witnessed three teenage girls congregating on the other side of the locked gate. Wearing the same standard-issue uniform as we had on, the three girls were wearing white cotton t-shirts and black sweatpants. The only difference was that their wardrobes were altered to appear as provocatively as possible, having cut the t-shirts just below their chests, each sporting a halter top with a torn deep V-neck, and unevenly hemmed sweatpants into short-shorts with the waistbands rolled up three or four times over.

Allowing Finn to greet the girls, who appeared confident in the face of the fairer sex, we kept our distance so as not to spook them with our awkward, inexperienced demeanor. Although Jim had only been fifteen at the time, giving him the right to bashfully avoid eye contact with the beauty that radiated through the bars of the entrance gate, I was nearly eighteen and had no excuse for acting just as intimidated. Admittedly at seventeen, I had not become a man in any definition of the term, which made females equally desirable as terrifying. Though I could portray the utmost self-confidence and extroversion when surrounded by like-minded boys, the introduction of a pretty girl would send me into a spiral of self-doubt and anxiety.

As Finn chatted with the three most beautiful teenage girls I had ever had the pleasure of avoiding, he instructed us to get closer.

"Get over here, you cowards. They won't bite," saying as the four of them laughed.

The girls held onto the bars of the gate, smiling at us as if we were skittish puppies they wished to pet. Finn suggested we be gentlemen and help our guests climb over the gate. Intimidated by the very thought of touching one of the girls' hands, in the most innocent of ways, I was simultaneously relieved and disappointed when the ring leader of the three girls took the initiative by removing her tailored t-shirt to throw it over the razor wire as a protective cover. Unabashed and brave with her beige brazier in plain view of our gawking gazes, the eldest of the three girls lifted herself over the gate, gliding over the torn t-shirt. She remained unscathed as she wrapped her small hand around a steel spike, then lowered herself to our side. Calling on us for some assistance like a damsel in distress as she underestimated the drop from the top of the gate, I summoned some chivalrous bravery from deep inside and placed my hands around her bare waist as she let her weight lean back on me. Having been the first time my inexperienced hands had touched the supple skin of a woman, I was embarrassingly aroused, forcing me to turn away from the appreciative girl without uttering a word. Cowering off to the side in an attempt to talk down the rising emotions that led to an inconvenient bodily reaction, I allowed Finn to assist the other two girls to scale the gate. Meanwhile, Jim was still staring into space as if he was identifying constellations rather than acknowledging the presence of such naturally beautiful young ladies.

Once they joined us on our side and retrieved the eldest girl's shirt from the snagging razors atop the mechanical gate, Finn introduced us to June, Autumn, and Daisy, collectively calling them the "three seasons." He assured us that although the fourth season was missing, she was in fact frigid and we had no need for her. Envious of his ability to evoke giggles from the three girls, I laughed along as I pretended to know the girl he was talking about. He continued the introduction by explaining that the three seasons were visiting from the Flint Valley camp for delinquent girls, adding an unnecessary, yet flirtatious adjective, referring to them as "naughty" girls. Flattered by their gratuitous laughter, Finn stood confidently as he introduced us, referring to me by my last name, Hunter, as he never bothered to ask my first name, then pointing over to Slim Jim, forgoing his nickname to Jim's relief, and introducing him more formally by his full name, James Wyatt.

As my heart sank into my stomach, weighed down by Slim Jim's last name as the anchor, I feared that he might have been of relation to my mother's disreputable family. Jumping to far-fetched conclusions while being provided with vague and limited information, I convinced myself that he had been another one of my mother's unwanted sons. Or, even worse, his abandonment could have been the result of Aunt Eleanor's irresponsible disposal of a vulnerable infant. I doubted my suspicion since Jim was visibly a different race than myself, scanning his mocha-colored skin and jet-black hair indicating he was in fact Hispanic, not just deceptively tanned from working outdoors in the pigment-changing, summer sun.

Privy of very little information regarding the suitors that frequented the beds of my mother and Aunt Eleanor, Jim's father could have been of Latin descent and had the misfortune of having a night of romance with either of the two. Looking for similar characteristics between Jim's and my family's genealogical traits, all born with almond-shaped eyes, a long, thin nose more suitable as a ski hill rather than a respiratory organ, and embarrassingly pointed ears making us all great candidates to play Santa's elves in school Christmas plays. Observing Jim for an uncomfortable amount of time, making my interest in the "three seasons" girls questionable, he did not possess any of my undesirable facial structures.

Despite Jim's symmetrically rounded ears, snub nose, and spherical eyes, I did not rule out the possibility that his biological father's genes were dominant, perhaps overshadowing the stagnant Wyatt gene pool. Since I didn't have a DNA test handy and I was caught staring at Jim's face more than once, I tried to enjoy the night spent with the girls from Flint Valley, especially June, whose uninhibited actions sent me into a frenzy of infatuation. Averting my socially inappropriate stare onto June instead of Jim, I caught her attention, subsequently flattering her into falling behind, choosing to walk next to me.

Taking the time to re-dress herself while I watched in awe,

June held her torn shirt in front of her to straighten it out, then tossed it over her head and fidgeted with it around her sun-kissed neck to shift it in the right direction. Realizing that no normal person should take that much time putting on a shirt, it became clear that her postponement of appearing fully dressed was merely to attract my attention. Wasting her time, my attention was undividedly hers and still would have been if she was wearing extra layers of clothes or even a parka. It was the beauty in her eyes that captured my attention, drawing me in like a sailor to a siren.

June put her shirt back on, only to stretch the neck of the torn collar over her shoulder to reveal her freckles closest to me.

"I got a pretty bad burn last week but now it's starting to tan," she said making conversation.

She then linked her arm to mine as Finn begrudgingly tried his luck by winning over the affection of Autumn upon noticing June's interest in yours truly. Walking in the dark clearing, with thousands of stars acting as our distant chaperones, Finn and I escorted our dates for the night toward my wooded boxing ring, as per my suggestion. Hoping to create a balanced portrait of sensitivity and raw masculine strength, I suggested that particular place knowing that the presence of the punching bag, a piece of manly athletic equipment, and Joe, a beloved dog, whose eyes would melt the heart of any boy or girl into a trusting trance, would paint me in a desirable light. Encouraging my suggestion of continuing the night in a secluded place away from the condemning eyes of Flint Ridge staff, Finn enthusiastically allowed me to lead the six of us through the forest.

Shrieking as the three girls were poked and prodded by unseen branches while feeling the prickly weeds brush against their soft ankles, they giggled with embellished fear, acting as if rodents were running into their socks. Reaching the rudimentary boxing ring, Finn jumped right in and started throwing punches to impress the girls, while Joe woke up from a peaceful nap and responded to his playful demeanor by jumping on him. Looking less impressive as he hollered for help to get Joe off his chest, pretending to be a worthy contender as his paws flailed against Finn's pectorals in excitement. Waiting a few seconds for Finn's humiliation to run its course, I eventually called Joe over to me and June, where we both applauded his obedience by ruffling his ears and scratching his belly. While we played with Joe, Finn brushed off both the dirt from his shirt and embarrassment from his ego, then went around the perimeter of the circle picking up various-sized rocks.

Haphazardly collecting stones, Finn filled his arms with a pile of them, proceeding to place them in a circle around the punching bag. Fully aware of his intentions with the rocks, I predicted that Counselor Arnold's punching bag would soon go up in flames. Although I knew the destruction of her property would be in poor taste, not to mention a slap in the face for all of the work she had already, and expected to, put in with me on the bag, I was still spiteful towards her egotistical priorities. Rather than consider the consequences of lighting a very flammable and large piece of vinyl, I was preoccupied with June standing by my side and preferred to entertain any option that would encourage her to get closer to me. Believing in the aphrodisiac powers of a campfire, I was fully invested in Finn getting that fire lit.

Once the irregular rocks were placed in what looked more like a rhombus rather than the conventional circular campfire shape, Finn began picking up twigs and leaves for kindling. As soon as he ran out of dry objects laying on the ground, he started ripping green branches from the encompassing trees instead of venturing into the dark forest for more suitable, dry wood. Not that he would have admitted it at the time, but he was fearful of accidentally grabbing a deceptively still snake.

Looking at the architectural disaster that was thrown underneath the hanging punching bag, I understood that there was a good chance Finn wouldn't be able to get the fire started, especially because we didn't have anything with which to ignite it. Weary of his abilities as a pyromaniac, I started thinking of alternative measures to woo June in case the absence of hypnotizing flames led her to boredom and subsequent disinterest in hanging around any longer. Averse to taking a walk in the unnerving pitch-black forest or blindly scaling the ridge, since I had lost my footing in broad daylight and having June watch me tumble down a hill was not ideal, I had hit a wall. Putting my hopes of June's affection in Finn's inept hands, I offered June a seat on a nearby tree stump, which was prime V.I.P. seating for the impending bonfire. Then, I walked over to the pile of forest debris and rearranged the branches to allow for air circulation on the off chance that one of us had something to light the potential fire.

Placing each flimsy twig and oblong branch vertically in a tee-pee style, I turned to Finn to ask him how he industriously intended on lighting the fire, or if he was waiting for divine intervention from the Greek god of teenage love. Responding with a confident, condescending smirk that indicated he had a hidden ace up his short, soiled sleeve, Finn picked up two of the particularly jagged rocks from the lop-sided campfire ring. He bent down to the inopportune kindling and rubbed the two stones together with swift force, causing brilliant sparks to spew from the colliding rocks onto the meticulously placed scraps of wood.

"You probably didn't know this, but Flint Ridge is named after all the flint rocks laying around," he said arrogantly.

Finn then continued to educate us on the local geological survey with an air of intelligence that captured the admiration of Jim's supposed date, Daisy. Latching on to whichever girl paid him the most attention, he indiscreetly locked eyes with Jim, shifting his vision over to Autumn, then back to Jim. Understanding the unspoken domineering order, Jim sauntered over to Autumn, leaving Daisy ripe for Finn's picking.

As Jim stood a foot from Autumn, nervously swaying side to side while looking up at the canopy of treetops to avoid unintentional eye contact with the auburn-haired beauty, Finn continued to rub the flint rocks together until a spark caught a dry twig, creating a flickering ember to form on the side of the make-shift tee-pee. Catching the dry leaves stuffed in the center of the kindling, white smoke began to billow from the pyramid of kindling. Impatient for raging flames to put our female guests in the mood for some anticipated romance, Finn counterintuitively blew on the smoldering ember, consequently blowing it out. As the cycle of rubbing the flint together, then blowing it out with a sexually frustrated breath, he continued to repeat his mistake until it was made apparent that the gaseous desperation in his breath was flammable.

Relieved by the single struggling flame that started to climb the bark of a green branch, the odds of putting our company into an uninhibited trance were greatly increased. Paired up as per Finn's self-interested partner assignment, we sat on tree stumps and oversized rocks around the pathetic fire, waiting in nervous anticipation of initiating intimate behavior. Even Finn, who portrayed a higher level of confidence than Jim and me, was just as catatonically frozen in his seat, unable to budge a single finger to caress Daisy's polished hand. Sitting in an awkward silence that could only be witnessed by observing a skittish group of overly self-aware teenagers, Finn thankfully broke the unspoken tension by suggesting we should smoke something.

"You girls smoke?" He said trying to sound nonchalant. "It really chills me out."

With an obvious ulterior motive, he alluded to the fact that smoking would ease our minds and relax our bodies, allowing us to enjoy the night with each other. Excited by the idea, the girls encouraged him to share the marijuana or tobacco he had been apparently withholding from the group but were confused and disappointed when he walked over to a birch tree and stripped a piece of white bark from the trunk. Holding a curled piece of birch bark in his hand, he walked over to a dying pine tree that was losing its needles from the summer's persistent drought. He gathered a handful of the brown pine needles, then placed them in a line at the center of the bark as if he was rolling a substantial joint. Once he fashioned the unusual smoking device, looking like a cheap white cigar, he bent down to the growing fire and lit the end of it. As some of the dried needles fell out of the brittle bark, catching fire and adding to the dwindling flame below, he puffed on it until it caught. Inhaling the pine-scented smoke, Finn held onto it like he was enjoying the high life, puffing on an expensive Cohiba.

Passing the bark/pine needle concoction to Slim Jim, he pursed his lips to the end of the birch bark. Indulging Finn's peer pressure, Jim accidentally inhaled the heavy smoke into his virgin lungs as he tried to keep the burning smoke in his mouth. Coughing worse than Lucille the lunch lady/intake worker, Jim passed the makeshift cigar to Autumn as he turned his head to keep from hacking on the lady to his left. Hesitant to smoke what had just suffocated Jim, Autumn intelligently skipped her turn and passed it over to me. Having bravely smoked the occasional cigarette in the faculty parking lot when I should have been in class, I did not have the same adverse reaction to the burning forest fragments as Jim had. Instead, I quite enjoyed the flavored smoke as I pretended that I was smoking one of Eleanor's menthol cigarettes I frequently stole. As I puffed away about a third of the birch bark, I then passed it to June with a smooth sophistication imitated from old nineteen-fifties private eye movies shown in class by aloof teachers. Politely declining my offer, she remarked that she would rather enjoy smoking something that would put her in a party mood.

Extinguishing the birch bark cigar on the side of the dew-soaked tree stump, and throwing it into the fire to fuel the flames, Finn let out a gasp as he watched me ruin his unsuccessful attempt at appearing suave. My peaking interest was directed at June as she reached down behind her torn t-shirt, grabbing her bra with both hands. Unsure as to what she was trying to accomplish but I was once again aroused by her unencumbered ways of exuding raw sexuality. Lifting her bra above her collar to get a closer look at the fabric covered underwiring, she tore the thread from an unevenly stitched seam, then placed the tips of her two fingers in the ripped seam. With an audience of three dazed, gulping teenage boys watching her every tantalizing move, she smiled as she retrieved a small joint from the padding of her bra.

Explaining that she had to hide it in her bra due to daily bunk checks by her Counselor following an unanticipated drug raid, she had been saving it for a special occasion. At the sight of the contraband joint, four out of the five of us eagerly awaited June as she took an elastic band that had been hanging on her wrist. Jim, however, looked terrified to partake in illegal activity. She then pulled back and tied her hair before bending over to light the joint on the intensifying campfire. Leaning her face towards the fire, within an inch of the chaotic blaze, her black bangs fluttered from the fire's heat as she ignited the marijuana. Helping herself to the first couple tokes from the joint, she filled her lungs with the psychotropic herb, then released a cloud of thick smoke. Before passing the joint to Daisy on her left, she grinned and looked me dead in the eyes.

If looks could kill, I would have been the most recent casualty of June's captivating hazel eyes. Acting more powerful than the effects of the drug I was about to experience, the luring gaze of a female was, and always has been, intoxicating. Entranced by her bloodshot eyes, I couldn't look away as my hyperactive libido wrestled my anxious mind into submission. Telling me to open my mouth, I followed her direction without questioning her motives, allowing her to guide me in whichever way she saw fit. I watched her intently as she breathed the inebriating smoke for twice as long as she previously did, then placed the joint between her index and middle finger before gently cupping my jaw with her tender touch. Guiding my face towards her own while resisting the burning reflex to exhale the potent smoke, she locked her lips with mine and exhaled the smoke into my mouth. Feeling as though we were sharing a single toxic breath, our airways connected to share the inebriating effects. Although my eyes were closed, I suspect that Finn and Jim were just as amazed as I was to see how fortunate I truly was.

    Feeling my heart race to a pace felt right before engaging in a fistfight, and my head spin as I had just stepped off a NASA centrifuge, I was not completely certain if my body was reacting to the THC in the marijuana or the sweet taste of June's glossed lips pressed up against my own. What started as a way to transfer the intoxicating smoke in an erotic manner, quickly turned into a passionate kiss. Even when the smoke dissipated, our lips remained locked, still enough to avoid misinterpreting the platonic moment as romantic. Following a few seconds of the chicken equivalent of kissing, I moved my lips. Luckily June reciprocated the affection and allowed me to continue kissing her, engaging in my first romantic encounter.

Witnessing my bold follow-up to an already impressive gift from June, Finn worked up the courage to kiss Daisy, who had been expecting him to do so after a series of movements that closed the gap between them. As Finn and I experienced paradise, located in a place opposing any interpretation of the subjective concept, I rudely opened my eyes for a second time to see if Jim had followed our lead by taking courageous action with Autumn. Intending to take a quick, hopeful glance at Jim, my stare lingered as he nor Autumn were anywhere in sight.

Equally astonished by his unpredicted absence and unsuspectedly high nerve, I was proud of Jim for taking a risk. Having spent enough time commending Jim in my mind and uninterested in Finn's indiscriminate conquests, I returned to enjoying my sensuous moment with June. It was a kind of passion that made me forget about the displeasing aspects of my life, both past and present; the ultimate escape that neither drugs, not alcohol could provide with such intensity and efficacy. Not only did I feel like I was being given an expression of undivided, pure love, but I was also able to show that kind of love to another person. Though I'm sure Joe enjoyed belly scratches as much as I enjoyed his playful licks, feeling a strong connection with another human being provided me with a type of invincibility. This invincibility, however pathetic, has been felt every time I've been given the chance to share an intimate moment with a partner since, especially my wife.

Although it would be storybook romance for my tale to end with June becoming my wife, detailing how we both used our love for one another as a reason to find a straight and narrow path that led to a happy marriage spanning several decades, resulting in the birth of three healthy children, the fact it that I never again saw June after that night. June was the first of many instant loves and would always be remembered as such, but I would have to wait well over a decade before meeting my true soulmate. She was worth the wait and I certainly enjoyed the sights along the way to meeting her, but as a seventeen-year-old, I didn't know the meaning of true love and obliviously, yet happily settled for the illusion of love.

Our night of passion never escalated beyond an innocent kiss and Finn never deflowered Daisy, although he liked to remember the night as being especially lucky for the year or so we stayed in touch following that summer. As far as I know, Jim's discovery of his own sexuality delved a bit deeper than my own, having enjoyed the privacy of being behind a faithful pine tree away from prying eyes, but maintained that he was completely respectful and did not push Autumn's comfort level. Despite the different levels of intimacy, and fabricated levels of intimacy in Finn's case, we were as happy as incarcerated teenage boys could be. In fact, we were so happy with our dates, exploring the uncharted landscape of blossoming romance, we were much too occupied that we were voluntarily blinded to our surroundings. Unfortunately, not a single one of us opened our eyes for the split-second it would take to notice that the dwindling campfire had caught the flammable vinyl punching bag above.

Only interrupting our respective make-out sessions once we felt the sweltering heat radiating from the scorched punching bag, Finn and I hesitantly left June and Daisy to try our hand at fighting the raging fire. As we frantically kicked and swatted at the burning bag, Joe simply basked in the heat that kept him warm from the chill of the night. Upon hearing our desperate hollers from combatting the spreading flames, Jim and Autumn halted their passion to see what had made us so frantic. Unable to keep the climbing fire from reaching the branch above, we watched as the current of heat from the red-hot punching bag blew the leaves off the treetops into the starry sky like a fiery leaf blower. Terrified of the uncontainable fire, we ran out of the forest, tripping on tree roots along the way.

Running for our lives, more scared of the punishment that would ensue after being fingered as the culprits of starting a forest fire than the actual fire itself, Joe followed our lead as a brisk wind fanned the embers. Unbearably hot for both humans and animals, we finally escaped the escalating fire and took a moment to catch our breaths. Coughing from the irritating smoke that billowed from the forest when I had been voluntarily smoking ignited pieces of the forest earlier in the night, I was unable to ask June if she was okay. The expression on her face answered the unasked question when she lost the angelic expression I had come to adore, having been replaced by unadulterated fear.

June's fearful reaction, which I assumed was in response to the confining fire, the cause of her sullen face was due to a much more threatening entity. Responding to my discomfort, Joe began snarling in the direction of our collective stare, ready to defend me from a predator. Wishing it had been a bear or wolf that was making its way toward a vulnerable pack of teenage prey, it was Mr. Desmond and his henchman, Paul: two significantly more vicious creatures.

Making their presence known by calmly walking up to us while talking nonchalantly about the terror they intended on unleashing, Mr. Desmond said,

"Paul, do you know what the punishment is for starting a forest fire?" He asked with a disconcerting calmness.

Acting coy, Paul responded, "No one has been stupid enough to warrant one but I'd happy to use my imagination and try it out on these three boys." He then shined a flashlight in our eyes. Commenting on our bloodshot eyes, Paul reported to Mr. Desmond that it appeared as though we had been indulging in an illegal substance. Content to hear that we had broken another rule warranting additional ruthless consequences, he walked up and peered into our eyes in judgmental agreement with Paul's keen observation. Noting that we had broken an exhaustive list of other rules, such as sneaking in unpermitted visitors, breaking curfew, and the most punishable offense, assault.

Cooperating as guilty offenders in regard to all of the listed transgressions, and identifying the futility of portraying an unbelievable innocence, we were confused as to the assault accusation. Turning to one another to see if we had somehow forgotten about a brawl that had transpired, we understood what Mr. Desmond was alluding to as he maliciously elbowed Paul in the face. Masochistically laughing in response to the planned attack, Paul wiped away the steady stream of blood running from the deep gash cutting through his right eyebrow. Realizing that we would be held accountable for the sociopathic actions of our maniacal director, I told June, Autumn, and Daisy to leave before things escalated and our superiors turned their ugly heads in their direction. Interfering with their desire to leave, Mr. Desmond held out his arm to keep them from fleeing, inappropriately placing his hand around June's bare mid-section.

"Where are you going, hunny?" He said inappropriately. "I assumed you were looking to have some fun tonight."

Leery of how far Mr. Desmond would be willing to go to assert his dominance, I stood in between him and June, once again insisting that the girls go back to the Flint Valley as I was the one who broke the rules.

"Let them go. I'll accept the punishment," I said bravely.

Confronting my intrusion as threatening behavior, Paul pushed me backward, away from Mr. Desmond. Unprepared for the violent shove, I was thrown off my feet and onto the ground, provoking Joe to bark in my defense. Aching from the impact with the hard ground, I could see from my flattened position on the ground that the fire had made its way to the perimeter of the forest, effortlessly scaling each tree.

Knowing we had little time before the entire camp was engulfed in flames with the assistance of the howling mountain winds, I needed to hastily find an escape route for the anxious girls being kept against their will by a violent captor. Perfectly in tune with my worried demeanor, Joe leaped forward from the shadows as our protector and began barking incessantly at Mr. Desmond and Paul. Looking down at the aging dog, Mr. Desmond remarked on yet another instance of insubordination, stating that pets were strictly prohibited. Indifferently commenting on the lack of animal shelters in the area, he turned back to Paul while holding on to June with one arm to ask if he could borrow his handy "dog muzzle." Recognizing the sinister inflection in his voice, Paul deciphered the true object his boss was requesting as he reached down to retrieve a pistol he had holstered on his ankle.

As the gun-shy canine fled in fear of the pistol aimed at him, Mr. Desmond changed the direction of the barrel to the second most defenseless thing in his presence. As he devilishly called Slim Jim over as he kept a tight hold around June, he waved the gun to express his impatience.

"Get over here, boy," he screamed.

Encouraging Jim to come closer, he continued to walk until the gun was pressed firmly against the scared boy's forehead. Instructing Jim to turn around, and face my direction, Mr. Desmond held the gun tightly with his finger pressed eagerly on the trigger, letting the barrel of the gun run alongside Jim's shaved head until it reached the back of his skull. Shouting at me to save him without saying a single word, Jim looked as though his life might have safer living on the harsh city streets. Responding to the welling tears in Jim's eyes as Mr. Desmond cackled, displaying an insanity fit for an asylum, my protective instinct kicked into overdrive. I lunged forward without a rational thought as to what I intended on doing. Since Counselor Arnold was not around to reiterate her "Foresight yields hope" mantra and my anger-releasing punching bag were incinerated, my uncaged anger was to be channeled toward Mr. Desmond.

Tackling the armed man to the ground, his arm flung into the air as he fired a shot into the sky. As he fell backward, his grip loosened on June, allowing her to escape without looking back to say goodbye. Watching from atop Mr. Desmond's aggressively flailing body, I could see the three girls run down past the main hall, down the road to the entrance gate, using the glare from the forest fire to light their way back to the girls' camp. Escaping one camp to safely return to another, I wondered if those girls ever got the chance to look back on that night as a whirlwind of twisted adventures or if they didn't get the same opportunity as I did to live long enough to recollect it with a heavy heart.

Assured that the girls were at least safe from Mr. Desmond and Paul's unquestionably malevolent intentions, I focused on wrestling the gun from Mr. Desmond's hand to ensure that Jim was out of harm's way. I hoped to save Jim like I wished I could have done for Lucky. Making sure that the night would not add to my haunting memories and instead provide me with redemption for past transgressions, I ignored Paul's striking blows to my back as I removed the gun from Mr. Desmond's stubborn, trigger-happy fingers. Before I could release his grip, another shot was fired over my head. Unable to see if Jim had taken the opportunity to increase his distance from the lethal altercation, I realized he had not been hit by the stray bullet when the blows to my back ceased instantly following the deafening blast from the gun.

Shocked by the sight of Paul's limp body falling to the ground behind me, Mr. Desmond realized his poor aim killed Paul, and was distracted long enough for me to wrangle the gun from his clenched hand. Gaining control of the weapon, I brought my quivering body to an upright stance, stepping over Paul's lifeless body while keeping my sights on Mr. Desmond. Laughing at me as I pointed the gun in his direction, he taunted me by snidely saying,

"You might be a stupid street kid, but I'm sure you're smarter than to kill a respected public figure," he said antagonizing. He then tried bargaining once he realized that my arms were as stiff as they were before he uttered the empty threat.

"All right, how about we forget all about tonight and we get you on a bus back home? How does that sound?" Speaking with an uncharacteristic quiver in his voice.

Unwilling to negotiate with the morally bankrupt director, I stood my ground and continued to contemplate my next move.

Mr. Desmond expedited my decision by switching his strategy from bargaining to threatening by saying,

"I will personally see to it that all three of you spend the rest of the summer at the bottom of The Pit without food or water until your organs fail."

He then lunged at me when the realization of his ineffective threats were falling short on my decision-making process. In a last attempt to save his own life, he used the only tool he had at his disposal: impulsive aggression. The same personality trait that allowed him to torment children was the one that ended his life as I reacted to his myopic stunt by pulling the trigger and firing a bullet in the center of his chest.

Gasping for air, it was evident that I had punctured his lung with hot lead, making it nearly impossible for Mr. Desmond to breathe. This would be the testimony the prosecution would later recount at my trial to a jury of twelve locals incapable of choosing between which fast-food restaurant they would order dinner from, let alone the fate of a recently turned eighteen-year-old stranger. Stunned by my short response time and limited rationale, I dropped the smoking pistol to the ground and ran after Jim and Finn, who had already gotten a head start as I considered the implications of my fatal actions.

As I ran as quickly as my trembling legs could carry me, I tried to calm down my horrified conscience by telling myself that I needed to save Jim's life. Believing that Jim's life was worth more than Mr. Desmond's based on moral character, the potential to provide benevolence in the future, and ridding the world of a little less evil, I justified my actions for a brief moment. Frantically running in opposite directions, I screamed out to the two boys,

"Behind the bunkers!"

Leading them to The Pit, Jim and Finn were trying to make sense of what they had just witnessed.

"What the hell were you thinking, man?" Finn exclaimed.

"You shouldn't have done that, Hunter," Jim said as he tried to hold back tears.

Questioning my impulsive behavior and accusing me of dooming them both to life in prison as accessories to murder, I ignored their off-handed remarks and kicked away a pile of lawn clippings and discarded branches before prying open the manhole cover.

Adverse to voluntarily subject themselves to time in the dreaded pit, I utilized a trick Counselor Arnold had shown me by pushing them into the hole without warning. As their shrieks lasted longer than their fall, it was apparent that the exaggerated perception of the depth of The Pit was not exclusive to my own distorted senses. I then made the short jump to the bottom of The Pit, accidentally landing on Jim's small, fragile frame. Forgetting to place the manhole cover back in its original position before landing at the bottom, I climbed back up the side of the stone wall, digging my fingernails over the jagged edges. Scaling the wall in what I would have considered record time if there had been such a competition, I struggled with the heavy manhole cover but eventually dragged it back in place with one hand as I hung onto the wall with the other like an extreme sports enthusiast dangling from a cliff. Allowing myself to fall back to the ground, again falling on Jim, who remained in complacent silence. Suspicious of the uncharacteristic silence that had befallen Jim and Finn upon hitting the bottom of The Pit, I worried that they had been injured. I was then corrected by Jim's disturbed gaze through the darkness of the tomb-like enclosure as his blank stare directed me to a child's lifeless body laying underneath my feet.

 We had solved the mystery of the missing Bunker Seven camper who had been last seen after receiving blunt force trauma to his skull courtesy of a tag team effort between Mr. Desmond's knee and the side of the Flint Ridge bus. Upon seeing such a gruesome sight, I at least felt relief knowing that I killed a man capable of murder and inhumanely disposing of a child's body. Although it only provided temporary relief, I embraced it as a comforting yet fleeting thought. Being stranded with the morose sight and feeling of a child's cold discarded body, we were unable to put into words how we were feeling. Instead, we kept our racing thoughts to ourselves and tried to make sense of how quickly a night of innocent fun could turn into a double homicide, the discovery of a missing boy, and causing a destructive forest fire.

As if we had remembered the presence of a raging fire closing in on us at the same time, we looked up at the loose manhole cover and started to feel the suffocating presence of carbon monoxide. Unable to muster enough strength amidst the lack of oxygen to remove the metal slab acting as a single, yet effective nail in our shared coffin, I came to terms with the possibility that my end was near. Hoping that Lucky wouldn't resent me for his death when we get reacquainted in the afterlife, I looked forward to hearing his foul-mouthed recount of the events leading up to his death. If there wasn't an afterlife and my existence was about to end at the bottom of that pit from smoke inhalation, I instead hoped that at least one person would remember me in a fond light, perhaps Counselor Arnold or even June, who could say a few nice words at my government-funded funeral at the nearby future site of the Flint Ridge cemetery for prisoners. Giving up on waiting for a saving grace, ready to offer my soul to any understanding deity or power that would have me, my life was extended as I could hear Counselor Arnold's voice calling out to us as he flipped over the manhole cover.

9

As I watched with great relief as Counselor Arnold reached down to pull us out of our chosen resting place, it felt as though I had relived those days at Flint Ridge in a matter of seconds. Breaking my trance as I heard the thud of the manhole cover echo in my reminiscent mind, it was matched by the sound of the heavy wooden door leading into the banquet hall. Forgetting for a little while about the purpose for my waiting in the hotel event room, I was reminded that I was about to reunite with the very people I had vividly been remembering in solitude. Wondering who the first guest was to enter through the doors, I lifted myself from the seat with curiosity. Unsure as to what I would say to any of the aged campers, my loss for words was lifted as I saw the unmistakable face of Slim Jim walking towards me.

Although he did not get any taller over the past fifty years, the nickname "Slim" was not entirely accurate anymore as he had acquired a spare tire around his midriff just as I did. To my relief, he was dressed in a similarly formal suit, which meant Finn could not focus the group's taunting at only me. Walking up to Jim, he greeted me with a smile and walked over to shake my hand. Dissatisfied by a handshake commonly shared by strangers and intermittent acquaintances, I threw my arms around him and squeezed him tightly. Reciprocating the same grip around my torso, I was assured that he was happy to see me as he said, "Nice to see you, big brother."

Commenting on his tardiness and unusual tendency to not follow protocol, he gave me a confused smirk as he pulled out the invitation he received indicating that the event started at seven o'clock. Looking down at my watch, it showed that it was precisely seven o'clock, realizing that I had somehow misread the invite, thinking I was supposed to arrive an hour earlier than expected. Lightheartedly slapping me on the back, Jim said,

"I guess I can forgive you since you saved my life all those years ago." Paused, then continued to say, "But I'm gunna hold you accountable next time."

I laughed and said, "I bet you will."
Sharing a chuckle, I scanned his face, noticing the same indicators of a long life lived, deep wrinkles, whitening hair, and unnaturally straight, false teeth. I basked in the uplifting thought that we were given the necessary time to develop such golden-aged, well-seasoned features.

As I told Jim how happy I was to see him, he told me that he had made a good life for himself, using his life experience and personal passion for helping homeless youth. He proudly mentioned that he recently had been working to help rebuild a local homeless shelter to expand its operations across the country, eventually building self-sustaining shelters all over the world. Hoping to directly help millions of struggling children escape the harsh environment of living without a place to call home, he offered kids just like his younger self the opportunity to pursue a prosperous life. One just like the life he had tirelessly built for himself. Admitting that I had not pursued such honorable endeavors, choosing to chase the almighty dollar than helping my fellow man, I instead shared pictures of my wife, two handsome sons, and a darling daughter. His eyes welled up with tears as he looked at the important people in my life and said with a raspy voice that he was happy to see I had found happiness after all these years.

As we reminisced about the not-so-good old days at Flint Ridge, I excitedly asked,

"Do you know if Finn is coming? I'd love to see that crazy bastard!"

As soon as Jim heard my question, he changed the expression on his giddy face to a solemn frown, understanding that it would be his morose job of informing me that Finn was no longer alive. Expecting to hear that he had suffered a fatal ailment that most men my age fear, like a heart attack, stroke, or any type of aggressive cancer, Jim explained why we wouldn't be seeing Finn on that or any other night.

"A few years after the Flint Ridge fire," Jim began to explain, "Finn overdosed in prison."

Saddened by the news of my old friend's death that had passed decades prior, I did not shed a tear for him. Not because I thought he deserved to die if he chose to gamble his life with narcotics or because I lacked empathy for a person in such unredeemable circumstances, but because I knew the reality of the uncertain fate surrounding the majority of teenagers subjected to toxic environments. I knew very well that Jim and I were the lucky exceptions to the disheartening rule of short lives for juvenile delinquents.

Pushing the conversation past the unfortunate news of Finn's passing, I did feel bad that I was not there for him even though I physically couldn't be at the time, but it did put our falling out into perspective. I only hoped that he knew I would have said a few nice words for him in his eulogy. After a moment of memory for our lost friend, we discussed what a relief it was to know that we were the last group of boys to be tormented by Mr. Desmond and Paul. We were also satisfied by the fact that they didn't live to regret crossing us that summer day. Morbidly raising a glass to their deaths, we laughed as I said,

"At least we made our quota…over twenty acres of forest cleared in a single night."

Finding my flippant comment amusing, he added,

"Yes. Twenty acres…And then some."

As we found out years after causing the fire that closed Flint Ridge for good, bunkers one through six were also torched by some equally careless campers in 2005; I just finished the job that had to get done to save future generations.

As we talked for hours, it was apparent that we were the only two former campers deranged enough to want to recollect the worst days of our lives. Using the encounter as much-needed closure allows us to look back on the trying times as merely an obstacle, not a defining time. Deciding together that we should get back to our rooms since we weren't young hooligans oblivious to circadian rhythms and needed the necessary sleep to function, we started to say our final goodbyes. Before leaving me, giving me one last hug, assuming that he would never see me again to get something important off his chest, he pulled back and sternly looked up into my eyes. Expecting him to have a last-minute change of heart and blame me for the chaos that ensued fifty years ago, I was surprised as he expressed his appreciation for my bravery in the face of Mr. Desmond and his gun.

He said, "Hunter, if you hadn't killed Desmond, not only would I not be standing here speaking to you, I wouldn't have had fifty years to actually enjoy my life. And for that, I am eternally grateful."

Unwilling to accept appreciation for committing murder, I simply said,

"Well old friend, I'm happy you're here too. But, I'd be lying if I said I didn't have a lot of regrets."

Nodding to acknowledge what I was alluding to, Jim asked if my time at Flint Ridge made me stronger, or even wiser. Thinking of an appropriate response to his loaded question, I looked down at my exposed wrist above the sleeve of my white dress shirt and contemplated as I read the tattooed words, "Foresight yields hope." After a moment of deep thought, considering the route my life took following that day, I replied by assuring him that I was both emotionally stronger and exponentially wiser than my seventeen-year-old self. Crediting the dearly departed Counselor Janis Arnold's wise words by which I lived my entire life with unwavering dedication, I said farewell to Jim for the second and last time.

Fixating on the events that resulted from acting on my impulsive urge to pull the trigger aimed at Mr. Desmond, I regretted not following Counselor Arnold's philosophy regardless of how much he deserved that fatal hole in his chest. I regretted not having the foresight to picture myself somewhere befitting a good-hearted person. I especially regretted not giving myself the benefit of the doubt, believing that there was hope for a discarded teenage criminal. As much as regret can provide a hypothetical reality in which life could have turned out better in a more timely manner, it is not a productive emotion. Despite it all, I truly believe that pulling the trigger, being convicted of murder, and subsequently spending fifteen years as one of the first inmates in the newly developed Flint Ridge Penitentiary gave me the discipline to rise above my inner struggle and bleak perception of the world. At least I was given parole due to the discovered body of the Bunker Seven child as evidence that I was being subjected to an abusive environment in a government-run facility. Most importantly, I did not and never will spend eternity resting at the bottom of a shallow, child-dug grave located in the arid, desolate valley of Flint Ridge.

Manufactured by Amazon.ca
Acheson, AB

15610192R00090